THE FURY OF STORMS

VOLUME TWO OF THE HELLEBORINE CHRONICLES

A novel by C.J. Pitchford

Illustrations by Marjorie Schott

Illustrated Trade Paperback Edition
ISBN-13: 978-0-9850882-5-5
ISBN-10: 0985088257

Also available:
iBooks Edition
ePub Edition

Published by Chris Pitchford Publishing, LTD

Play the games "Airship Agility Free," and—coming soon—"Airship Fury Free," available on the App Store.

Dedication

I gratefully dedicate this book to my step-mother, Ellen, for all that she has done for our family, and to my sister, Leslie, for all that she is doing for her own family.

Gratitude

I am, of course, deeply indebted to the editor of this work, Karen Conlin, via http://grammargeddon.com, for all her incredible work. (Yet, any mistakes still found in this volume are entirely mine, and mine alone. Sorry about them)...

This book simply wouldn't be before you now without the encouragement of Kristine Shafer, the keeper of my heart and the voice of Seramis Helleborine. I wish to congratulate my daughter, Kate, on all that she has accomplished. I'd like to thank my mother for her support. And speaking of support, thanks, Dad! (The kickstarter wouldn't have been a success without you...)

And speaking of the kickstarter...

Thank you, Stephanie Buday, Kendra Schott, Kathy Fletcher, Clayton Thurgood Bigsby III (quite possibly not his real name), Jennifer Rose and Joshua Hill!

Epigram, with a note by the author

Vital spark of heavenly flame!
Quit, O quit this mortal frame:
Trembling, hoping, lingering, flying,
O the pain, the bliss of dying!
Cease, fond Nature, cease thy strife,
And let me languish into life.

Hark! they whisper; angels say,
Sister Spirit, come away!
What is this absorbs me quite?
Steals my senses, shuts my sight,
Drowns my spirits, draws my breath?
Tell me, my soul, can this be death?

The world recedes; it disappears!
Heav'n opens on my eyes! my ears
With sounds seraphic ring!
Lend, lend your wings! I mount! I fly!
O Grave! where is thy victory?
O Death! where is thy sting?

Alexander Pope, "Vital Spark of Heavenly Flame,"
From *The Spectator* (May 14, 1712)

Samuel Willoughby Duffield, in his *English Hymns: Their Authors and History*, refers to the text above as "an extract from the *Messiah*, which is a rendering of the *Fourth Eclogue* of Virgil." The last couplet is a re-working of 1 Corinthians 15:55, a discussion, one presumes, of immortality.

Table of Contents

Prologue: Academic Questions

From a journal, author unknown (believed to be Seramis Helleborine, GCB, Marchioness of Cambridgeshire; corroborating documents to follow).

I had gone to war and lost. I had no idea what I was supposed to do, and nothing quite reinforces that sense of personal futility like standing upon the deck of an airship that is falling out of the sky. For one brief moment I took solace in the gentle touch of that noble lord, Henry Albion. But I cursed myself for a misbegotten fool when my ship, *The Agility of Clouds*, dropped from underneath us, careening down through the air straight into the sea near Bermuda below.

Even now, I can see the combination of pride and pain in my words, and a part of me still fails to understand why this would be so. After months of planning and designs, I had conceived how to transform a sailing vessel into a flying ship and then carried out that transformation. I had literally risen above the storms that buffeted us and then had flown victorious over the remains of the aerial armada that had attacked us. But two dead bodies stained the deck with their blood and the author of this war had disappeared quite literally into thin air.

The sweet taste of my so-called victory had turned to ash in my mouth as I stumbled, and I would have fallen if not for the kindness and support of my dear Henry, Lord Albion. But[—]

Patrick Tempus, now a phantom known as Father Time, had once been a tool of one of the bodies lying lifeless upon my ship: the Lord De La Warr. Lord De La Warr, once the Baron Thomas West, had also been my patron and family protector—my Nuncle—as I grew up orphaned but not alone. I see now the reason for his generosity, as when disaster first befell my household he was there—not to help rather to arrest me for witchcraft and set in motion a scheme to find the author of the plans that inspired the vessel upon which he died.

One of Father Time's minions, a contemptible lad named Innes slew Lord De La Warr. Innes, who tried to use me like a tool, and when given the opportunity, violently kidnapped me...

But he, too, is dead. Slain by Lord De La Warr in my protector's final act, as such, of defending me. Thus was the cost of war, and even as I write these words days after the fact, I can't fathom what was the reason for such madness.

My head throbs. Time slows almost to a stop as I try to recall just why[—]

I apologize for the interruption, but I couldn't continue writing.

A night's sleep has cleared my senses but not given me any clarity as to what Patrick Tempus—Father Time—had hoped to achieve through his rebellious acts. It's as if he, too, were a pawn set in motion by some players who haven't revealed themselves as of yet. I fear I may be much too deep within a violent game played by rules I can neither comprehend nor countenance. However, not for myself do I worry, but for the others I can see as plain as if they stood here now before me as I recall the terror of falling through the air.

For it was while falling and while lost in uncertainty that I witnessed such bravery, such raw belief as I had never before experienced. Captain de Ibarra, a Privateer under the English flag in an earlier part of his career, had one firm hand at the wheel and another on his feathered tricorn. His wink of reassurance was meant to comfort me, I am sure, but he seemed to be taking as much solace from me as I was from him. Hanaawa, the war chief of the Natchez, was assisting the crew in tying down spars that had come loose as the wind thrashed about us. His broad, brown face never wavered despite the clear sense amongst all that the ship was doomed. Also his niece, White Apple, never left her post in the crow's nest despite the pitching and swaying of the craft as it fell. Her clear, high voice rang out above the shouts of the crew as she noted our descent, a countdown that never faltered despite the danger.

The Fury of Storms

They are all gone, now. But I do not mean that we had crashed. I have not even been able to explain what had caused such turmoil in the first place. Of course, the airship is able to float upon the wind using a compound derived from pitchblende, an element that is itself lighter than air. By amassing a quantity of the gas within an airtight container of sufficient volume, the resulting forces of equilibria counter the gravitational effects and thus, we fly.

But I have witnessed another force that was able to counter the effects of gravity, seen only from a distance and most certainly without the least bit of comprehension on my part. Before my disbelieving eyes, brilliant lights twisted and rushed about a chasm in the island of Bermuda. Like ghostly flaming hands, the inexplicable forces had compressed and carved a column out of the earth and thrust it into the sky to a height beyond measure. I can see, it, too, as plain as any before me, but I take no comfort in the vision. In fact, it terrifies me unreasonably. But only so much as I still take no solace in its disappearance, for as soon as Father Time had disappeared from sight, the towering column of earth exploded. It was that blast that had sent *The Agility of Clouds* swerving through the sky. But at the last moment, just before we were to drop into the ocean, the wings of the aerialwave finally bit into the air with intended purpose and dropped us all gently upon the rolling waves, as if to mock our efforts and my uncertainty as being mere trivialities in comparison to the forces of fate that were our destiny.

However, even now the effluvia and detritus of the shattered column of earth spread across the skies over the Atlantic Ocean, casting a gloom upon the sea. I wonder if the gloom has reached Colonel and Mrs. McClure back at New Helleborine Hall in Virginia. Sadly—as I sit alone writing this—that is where I've sent Captain de Ibarra, Hanaawa, and White Apple.

Truly, I have sent them away for I have become death. I am doomed, and my doom is casting down all about me.

From Acting Captain Viscount Archimedes Smythe's Duty Log,
HMS Royal Sovereign, 21 December 1730

I must first and in all fairneſs note that I do not believe that these words in any likelihood will ever be sene by the eyes of mortal men, but that I record the truthe here just as I have witneſsed it, so help me GOD, &c.

The Fury of Storms

The Lord De La Warr, reſt his soul, had taken charge of the Atlantic Squadrons in HIS MAJESTY'S ROYAL NAVY, but Lord Admiral Duke Albion of Glouceſter, as always, was in actual command of the ships. They sought a marchioneſs, the Lady Helleborine of Cambridgeshire, who was transported under myſterious circumſtances to the Colonies. While the orders I receiv'd were vague on that point, they were completely and unqueſtionably clear on another target: a rogue spy called Patrick Tempus. He was to be regarded as heretical and extremely dangerous. Yet, I think he may even be beyond all that, now.

But I digreſs.

We sailed north of the Thirties, so progreſs was slow to PORTSMOUTH, Virginia Colony. There, we diſcovered that the Marchioness had staked a claim, built a homeſtead and mill, and further, had purchaſed a ship and purſued the villiane, who had reportedly taken on another persona, calling himself Father Time.

Our mission chang'd to one of reſcue, but it was not long before we needed succor ourselves. Again, I'm getting ahead of my report, as firſt we had followed her Ladyship down the coaſt of the New World, almost to SAINT AUGUSTIN in Spanish Florida. We just miſsed the capture of the rogue spy, but were able to reſcue the marchioneſs. For her pains, the Lady was knighted and made a Dame Commander of His Majeſty's own Order of the Bath. I will always remember her appearance upon the Royal Sovereign. Her faire hair and gracefull bearing were out of place on the warship. Her delicate frame made her seem small and almoſt inſignificant.

But the next time I saw her, she was sailing through the skies in a veſsel of her own designe. As I mentioned previouſly, we had needed reſcuing becaus we had become trapp'd within a hurricane that had stopp'd in time. I swear that I am writing the truth, just as I witneſs'd it. I wouldn't believe what I had sene, had I not sene it for myſelf. And I would not be here at all as the hurricane was quite deadly, deſpite being unmoving. The Dame Commander flew her ship, THE AGILITY OF CLOUDS, right into the eye of the hurricane, and then led us all on the Royal Sovereign to safety.

We had reports that His Majeſty's ships had disappeared in the Atlantic, and that all contact with Bermuda had, in fact, been loſt. While the 'airship' flew in front of us, we lumber'd behind them in awe and wonder till coming upon an aerial flotilla at Bermuda led by FATHER TIME. Of a different and apparently inferior designe to that created by the Dame Commander, more than a dozen veſsels took to the aire. The slight and graceful Dame Commander fought them all, and was victorious.

But her victory was not without cost. I was placed in command of the Royal Sovereign while Lord De La Warr and Admiral Albion joined in an attempt to capture the rogue spy. Sadly, Lord De La Warr was loſt in the final attack, struck down by a minion of the heretic. And somehow, in a manner not fully underſtood or articulated, Father Time escap'd. It is said that he simply disappeared from sight. Of cours, I had all this second-hand, as I was still aboard the Royal Sovereign. However, I report it heer, as it happen'd on my watch.

But that was not the worſt nor moſt unexplainable event during my brief tenure in command of HIS MAJESTY'S FLAGSHIP. My feble powers of description faile me despite being able to close my eyes and see the tower of earth cleare as day. An inexplicable towering column of earth had grown straight up into the sky diſappearing at a height beyond sight. By itself, it would be maybe nothing more than a curioſity; it certainly wasn't much to look at, besides being a thin straight line that diſappeared from sight. But upon the diſappearance of the villaine, it exploded. In my experience with the great volcanos, ash plumes that go high enough can spred over an entire region. When this mysterious column of earth spred its debris in all directions, I could see no limit to the darkneſs to follow.

—Retrieved from Royal Nautical Museum Archives, 22 June 2014

Translated from the transcribed oral history of Elder Octochay,
Recorded ~250 years prior to present day, Natchez Nation

When the sky darkened and the pale demons were purged from our lands a great awakening came upon our people. Our Great Mother Sun had returned in human form at the end of great tribulations. And for a while all the people in our land were as one.

The Fury of Storms

But before that great awakening one pale demon with eyes of fire had united many nations in a purpose terrible and unclean. War against the European colonists gained our people freedom at a horrific cost. Yet, not everyone dreamt the dream of war.

My people of the Natchez had been driven from our homes when we refused to join with the pale demon. We suffered when we honored the agreement we had with the English. But it was an English woman called Seramis Helleborine who gave aid and assistance to me and other survivors when we were chased by the pale demon's allies.

The pale demon with eyes of fire brought war to our shore. But the devastation of war was nothing like the transformation wrought afterwards by the return of the Great Mother Sun.

— As accessed in the People's Archives,
6 Rabbit 2559 VB
(*Varshha Bodhisattva* [Year of our Lord, Buddha])

PART ONE: The World,
Split Into Two

A toy promises more than just diversion.

Chapter One: A Parting

In which our players depart in different directions

The explosion produced a shock wave that temporarily distorted even the clouds, rippling through tropical water vapor at the speed of sound. The towering column of earth that had been consuming the island of Bermuda and had grown tall beyond sight had exploded in a furious storm of incomprehensible power. Without mercy, the results of the devastating blast concussed the crew of the improbable airship, *The Agility of Clouds*. Despite being able to perceive the effects with ten times the detail as anyone else present, the woman responsible for its flight—Seramis Helleborine—also reeled and fell before recovering and taking the wheel herself.

At first, the enhanced and repurposed *caravel redonda* was buffeted in all directions, out of control while floating— sinking, really—towards the much larger British man-o-war of the first rate anchored off the island's coast, His Majesty's Flagship, *Royal Sovereign*. The ropes binding the large envelopes of lighter-than-air gas to the airship seemed to stretch nearly to the breaking point, while the dozens of mechanical wings on each side of the vessel tore at the air in futile gestures. Hundreds of sailors on the Royal Sovereign, who owed their lives to the previous heroic actions of the daring airship and her Dame Commander, stood in silence, fearing that *The Agility of Clouds* would crash.

When the initial blast subsided, however, both crews had recovered and had resumed control of their vessels. All around them, the formerly clear blue skies and seas vanished behind clouds of detritus and earth, and it appeared that the world would never be the same again. Bermuda was now enshrouded in a gloomy shadow as the dust and rubble drifted away from the explosion of the column that had consumed much of the land in its inexplicable growth as it sprouted from the island. Trade winds high in the atmosphere dispersed the particles mainly towards Europe, but the sheer mass of the clouds also spread towards the mainland of the New World.

For her part, when she could pause in her struggle at the wheel of the airship, Seramis looked at the growing clouds and, in shock at the hellish transformation, felt herself pulled in each direction, despite first requiring she survive the fall from the sky before she would need to choose.

Captain de Ibarra recovered and, thanking his employer and friend, once again took the wheel. After adjusting his tricorn and patting down his velvet waistcoat, he called out for assistance, rousing the crew to their stations. His rough voice sounded thin to Seramis, although she thought it might be the ringing in her ears that caused that effect.

The Natchez chief, Hanaawa, and his niece, White Apple, also recovered quickly. But the advantage went to youth, as White Apple returned to the crow's nest first to guide the captain to ground. Indeed, the rest of the crew of the Agility were soon at their stations, and all were looking to their leader, the Dame Commander Seramis Helleborine, for direction—yet finding none.

Wordlessly, each of her friends approached in turn but left in silence, as she would neither speak nor meet their imploring expressions. They quietly undertook tasks of their own, leaving Seramis silent in her sorrow. Reverently, they also attended to the immediate sources of her pain: the bodies of those slain who would no longer feel anything, who lay upon the deck in violent repose. Upon the airship's gentle landing on the darkened waters, Lord Admiral Albion sadly took his leave and resumed command of HMS *Royal Sovereign*.

Unexpectedly, Seramis followed Albion, and in fact had taken upon herself the role of surgeon's assistant in the disposition of the bodies of the two men who had harmed her most in life, the murderous Innes and the scheming Lord De La Warr. Despite her shock at the deaths of these two men, she had taken charge of the transfer of their bodies to the *Royal Sovereign* from the *Agility* where they had swiftly clashed and died.

The surgeon of the flagship, for his part, largely ignored the silent marchioness with a studious air he had cultivated while ignoring those screaming in pain and groaning in supplication. Both of the deceased had already bled out, so the surgeon carefully removed and discarded their clothes while Lady Seramis modestly and passively watched the spreading gloom, despite the bells of the watch sounding midday.

Orderlies brought fresh clothes for Lord De La Warr and canvas to wrap the body of Innes, a shroud for his impending burial at sea. They then poured lead shot into Innes's abdominal cavity before wrapping him, to ensure his sinking to the depths of the ocean. But before they could complete the wrapping of his head, Lady Seramis interrupted them, and looked one final time upon the man who had violently betrayed her.

Innes's face, passive and unreadable in death and reflecting the emptiness that had once been within him, felt cold to the touch. Just as he had once been an empty vessel of Patrick Tempus to be filled with whatever ambition the master desired of his slave—so, too, were his features now empty; his face revealed nothing to Seramis's searching gaze.

Silently, she said good-bye to the first man to whom she had opened herself. Thus, she said good-bye to her innocence, a concept defined now only in its absence. Briefly, visions of their time together flooded her sight, filling her eyes with a picture of laughter. But that, she now knew, had been mere pretense. The last scene that she remembered, the one that she would carry always, was the mental image of Innes calmly raising his flintlock pistol in betrayal.

While the orderlies completed roughly wrapping Innes for his burial in the miserable twilight, the surgeon had finished the first stages of embalming Lord De La Warr using camphor and myrrh. Just before the surgeon was to set the deceased's features for the journey back to England, Seramis coolly and quietly interrupted the process.

She expressionlessly looked at the stern features of her former patron and Nuncle, which even in death appeared strong yet pained. She had once feared him as a powerful patron, and had even recently despised him for his own betrayal of promises made. But for all that, she couldn't bring herself to condemn the man who had so evidently cared for her and had even died in her defense.

Her head started to throb, almost as a physical manifestation of the warring feelings within. Her head was indeed filled with unresolved issues, the questions she still carried about her patron and how now none of that would ever be directly resolved. A gasp of pain and frustration escaped from Lady Seramis's lips, quickly summoning the duke of Gloucester, who had been busily performing his duties within a discreet distance.

"Milady, if you wish to return to your craft, I will have the launch readied—" His eyes were wide with concern and his jaw set in determination.

"Your Grace—" Lady Seramis interrupted but was stopped by his raised gloved hand. His uniform was as crisp as his gestures, she thought.

"Please, call me Henry." His smile was warm and sincere.

Her answering smile was brief, and her eyes shone with tears. "This disaster was my doing, but I'm afraid that I haven't the resources to try to set things right—"

"I will be so bold as to disagree with both assessments, milady." He smiled.

Seramis wanted very much to lose herself in that smile, but the pain within was too much. Her head drooped—a little—as if her heart were heavy and pulled her down with its weight.

She responded only with formalities. "Can you send a summons to the captain and officers of the *Agility* for a conference?" She spoke as if being Dame Commander were as natural as any other role she had been asked to perform.

Turning to his left, Albion spoke curtly. "Lieutenant? Just as ordered by the Fleet Captain."

"Aye, sir," said the officer, who then departed as if the very model of efficiency.

"A garrison officer has taken charge in Bermuda, Commander," the admiral said, responding to her in kind. "But we have no further intelligence as to the plans of Patrick Tempus or how he could have simply vanished into thin air. There is obviously so much more going on here than I can hope to understand. Would you agree that it seems that even as one mystery is solved, two more are as quickly revealed?"

Seramis breathed deeply, her gloved hands clasped in front of her. "I'm so sorry that I ever involved you in this," she said. "My vendetta against Innes and my clashing with Lord De La Warr have brought this disaster upon us all—"

"How can you shoulder the responsibility for such a plot beyond reckoning? When all that has been wrought by another?" His voice softened in gratitude and appreciation. "I'll remind you that you've once come to my rescue and saved me. A hurricane—frozen in time—would have been my undoing, if not for you." Louder now, as his emotions took hold, he went on. "Patrick Tempus styled himself Father Time, but the frozen hurricane, the pillar of earth, and now this perpetual gloom are clearly beyond any one person's doing."

Arriving far sooner than Seramis expected, White Apple stepped forward gracefully and asked with a precocious grin, "Even by someone who can disappear at will, Your Grace?" She had just arrived from the *Agility* with the dapper Rogero Francisco de Ibarra y Valdez and the stoic Hanaawa, who gently shushed his niece.

Captain de Ibarra, commander of the airship Seramis had herself designed, bowed deeply to Lady Seramis. "We were, of course, ready for your request, Fleet Captain." His gaze then became defiant. "I assume that because you haven't returned to the *Agility*, you're staying here on this bucket—"

"Your intelligence and pride are revealed in equal measure, Captain," the admiral interrupted.

"Gentlemen," Seramis chided gently. "First, what is the status of the *Agility*, Captain?"

"Ready to depart for any destination on the globe you may wish, Fleet Captain," de Ibarra answered proudly with a flourish of his tricorn.

She nodded in acknowledgement. Turning to the Natchez war chief, Seramis looked at her friend imploringly. "I admit I'm at a loss to explain what has happened here. Hanaawa, your insights have proven their worth before. Is there anything that you can tell me?"

"I can only point out what your eyes already tell you," he said. His gaze sought an unseen middle distance. "Daylight is gone from this part of the world. Eventually it will return, as that is the way of things. But, in the meantime, there will be famine, death, and bloody conflict over diminishing supplies and resources, as that, too, is the way of things." He turned to White Apple, who had uttered a small sound of distress.

"We must warn them," she blurted, not needing to explain who she meant by 'them'—the families and the colonists who joined together at New Helleborine Hall— before reaching out to Seramis. "But I don't want to go! I... I wish we could have had that conversation you mentioned earlier, milady." She spoke quietly, referring to the promised but now delayed discussion of life's many changes.

"I'm so sorry," Seramis said as emotion filled her voice. "But we will have that conversation, someday, I swear."

She paused, wondering whether she would be able to keep that promise. "You're correct about raising the alarm, White Apple. In the meantime, I want to ask you to use your keen eyesight to watch over your uncle and your captain."

White Apple nodded, evidently not trusting herself to speak. She looked down at her hands folded in front of her.

Lady Seramis placed her hand on the maiden's shoulder, pausing as she struggled with what to say next. "I have to go to England to warn the king and ask for his assistance in dealing with this disaster. But Captain de Ibarra, you, and the others must go to Virginia Colony and find out what you can about that so-called Father Time. He may have vanished, but I fear we will see him again even as we seek the answer to what has happened here and to who is really behind all that has befallen us." She gestured to the dark clouds above her.

"I thought it might be so, milady," Captain de Ibarra said sadly as he removed his hat. "So I've had your maids gather your things, and they're here aboard this bucket as well."

"Please ask one to stay, and the others should return with you to assist Mrs. McClure. She will need the help if Hanaawa is correct in his assessment of humanity's follies and shortcomings," she said. Breathing deeply, she steeled herself against the pain of separation and loss that she already felt.

Hanaawa smiled a weak smile as he visibly struggled with his conflicting emotions. "I wish I could be faulted for overestimating the follies of humanity, as you have so eloquently put it, but first I have two questions. What do we do should we actually uncover the truth behind Father Time?"

He paused, knowing that there wasn't yet an answer. Looking at Seramis, he asked another question that had no answer as well. "And does anyone have any idea what we can possibly say to Colonel McClure when he realizes we've returned to New Helleborine Hall without you?"

Father Time, once known as Patrick Tempus in a mundane existence ill-suited to his current situation, stared through incorporeal eyes in disbelief. He never imagined the scene before him, a daytime sky so black, a sun so bright, a globe so round and yet much smaller than he imagined. The heart in his breast may no longer beat, but he cared not as he surveyed the hemisphere at his feet.

He had himself become much larger than he would have ever thought possible. On two ghostly legs he stood astride the Eastern Seaboard of the North American continent. He had seen maps of the great Atlantic Ocean, but now if he wished he could stretch his arms to point to the African shore itself, thousands of leagues away in a vision that Father Time never before imagined.

As quotes from the Bard filled his mind, one stood out:

> *"And I will purge thy mortal grossness so*
> *That thou shalt like an airy spirit go..."*

The Fury of Storms

Poor Bottom never stood so tall, never towered over so much as this, Father Time thought.

A hurricane in the western Atlantic—frozen in time by his early experiments, its clouds arranged in neat concentric circles—attracted his attention. Father Time was aware of his hands although he could not see them as such. He leaned over and brushed his fingers through the hurricane, setting it back into motion. He spun it faster and faster until the clouds dissipated before his sight, becoming as intangible as he himself had become.

But what, exactly, had he become? He no longer knew what he was. Although he didn't feel different, it was quite obvious that he was no longer the same. His senses were unchanged, as he could see the planet's rotation in the motion of the stars... He was surprised that the sunset occurred so quickly (there was no dusk to speak of—merely a wink, and the sun was gone), followed by a multitude of stars exploding, unblinking, into existence upon the night sky.

He could feel his body—that is, the proprioception of where its various parts were located—but he could experience neither warmth nor cold, no texture nor any other kind of touch. And, as with the hurricane he had once stopped in its tracks, he had no idea how this had come to be.

"*Confusion now hath made his masterpiece*," he whispered aloud. And MacDuff would have said the same now as he had in the Scottish play by the Bard. But where the original line had been spoken in horror, Father Time smiled at the recollection of the murder of Lord De La Warr.

Laughter at the realization of his ascension and his magnitude poured forth from Father Time, heard by none but felt as an unease in the nightmares of all who slept and dreamt that night. Father Time's vision twisted in his mirth, and a rumbling under his feet suggested that his predicament was far from stable, intimating that he was as he was only by his will alone.

"I have done it!" he shouted in an exulted voice that he could only sense, but not hear.

"No, we have done it," answered a cold, spectral wind. "We have journeyed across the millennia in order to change conditions on this planet to our desires, and you are our instrument."

There was no one source to the voice; seemingly, it came from everywhere. It filled him. It infused the whole of the immense specter he had become. "We become impatient with our tool," the voice continued. "Time, in this scale, moves quickly, as you can see."

"I had hoped! O Masters of Mysteries, truly, had I hoped I would attract the higher beings from my dreams—" Father Time began in earnest.

"It was not you who attracted us, but instead, we who have been manipulating you"—haughty and insouciant, the voice was terrifying and yet appealing to Father Time—"for a task of our own design: one which you cannot accomplish standing here while time flies before your eyes."

Indeed as the voice described, the sun burst forth above the eastern horizon in a dazzling magnificence that burned the stars from sight and transformed the cold globe into a lighted sphere. But the sphere was no longer shiny blue and green and white as it might have appeared, as there was a stain growing from Bermuda which, though it lightened somewhat as it spread, yet plunged the world beneath it into shadow. Even at this height the menacing cloud was settling and dissipating, as if being poured into the lower atmosphere.

"You notice our handiwork," the voice continued. "We have traveled from what you would call the five-hundred-and-tenth century in order to remake this world into something more to our liking. But you are not simply witness to the chaos and destruction that is to follow. You must eliminate the potential challengers to our supremacy."

Then a pause, and a rage within him erupted as he thought of another who had replaced him in his former employ as a spy for Lord De La Warr. The thought occurred to him, burning through his brain, that she might have been manipulated, too; and further, she would supplant him if possible! "I know of whom you speak! And I shall tear her apart as she burns!"

"You cannot—confront her directly," the voice chided, but sounding less sure of itself than previously.

"Why?" Father Time screamed in a voice without sound, having seized upon the thread of possibility the voice refused to weave into existence. "I am not to be caged. I stand at the pinnacle of volition. The very substance of existence bends to my will."

"While it is possible for primitives like you to aspire and even—in some rare cases, attempt—manipulations such as we dispense, for those we have manipulated, we decree that there can be no conflict. You will not be allowed to directly challenge any we have uplifted, just as they cannot directly diminish you in any capacity."

"I don't understand," he shouted. "You must know that I follow no rules save my own! Who can stand before me? You've made me a god!"

"We will unmake you if you do not pursue our will." As the last word faded, fires of ethereal poison erupted behind Father Time's eyes, melting his thoughts and willpower, leaving naught but pleas of supplication. In an instant, the fires had burned out, and Father Time was left wordless, stunned and humbled before his gods.

When his voice returned, the question "What will you have me do?" was almost all that was left. Almost—except for one tiny fire that didn't go out. One spark within Father Time, hidden and controlled, but burning and containing the potential for uncontrolled conflagration, for the destined redemption of supremacy.

Simply put, for revenge.

Chapter Two: A Proposal

In which our heroine is lost between two worlds

Ill winds buffeted HMS *Royal Sovereign* as it traversed the cloud-covered Atlantic. The ship was tossed about by storms where the normally steady Gulf Stream becomes the North Atlantic Drift. The changed climate mirrored the storms of anxieties and worries that Lady Seramis tried in vain to suppress with a daily routine of experiments, calculations, and writing.

But events and routine both conspired to wrest her from her self-imposed schedule. When the body of the traitor Innes was consigned to the deep, she silently attended the ceremony, as the storms couldn't keep her from seeking closure. Lady Seramis was the only one present who had known him. But she realized that she hadn't really known him at all. She had poured into him a history of her own imagining and had taken his words of manipulation as sincere.

Later, she attempted to write all that she'd known of him, and didn't get beyond a single, short list. In comparison, she wrote down all she had shared with him—her confessions, aspirations, inventions, and stories—and marveled at how it filled the page. Her ink-stained fingers now bore accusations of her naiveté, and she washed and rewashed her hands as if to remove her own sorrow and guilt.

Lady Seramis spent each day within the admiral's stateroom of the *Royal Sovereign* ignoring those who knocked in vain at her cabin door. She knew she had been much more successful at hiding her own talents and her slow-drifting passage through time when she had not been so distraught and self-absorbed.

Unfortunately, her instructions to her maid and the crew of the flagship became an ever more swiftly moving stream of almost unintelligible vocalizations that only repeated transcriptions and interpretations could begin to decipher. Alice, Lady Seramis's maidservant, had become gradually accustomed to the verbal eccentricity of her mistress. In sympathy if not outright exasperation, Alice would shush inquiries and shoo away the officers who requested Lady Seramis's attention, and pass along the marchioness's instructions as she could best understand them.

Seramis's work kept her within the stateroom, except for the times when the weather subsided and her maid's enforced constitutionals took her above deck. During those times, usually cloaked and cowled, her appearance was deeply mysterious if not actually unnerving to the sailors who weren't able to discreetly remove themselves from the dame commander's path.

Wearing a hat she had modified with various jeweler's loupes and magnifying glasses on numerous swiveling and articulated posts so that they might be positioned and re-positioned as needed, Seramis was rebuilding the combination chronometer and gyroscope she had first created as an aid in navigating her airship, *The Agility of*

Clouds, when the admiral, Duke of Gloucester, Henry Albion was announced.

He was direct. "Milady, what fever possesses you?" Alice exited the stateroom, leaving them alone, the demands of decorum losing when weighed against the needs and well-being of her mistress.

Concern sharpening his handsome features, he stood in the yellow light of the lamps awaiting her response, but none came. Across the gulf of their fears, the two stared at each other, until he spoke again. "I'm very truly worried for you, milady. What might I do? Ask me anything..."

Blinking rapidly at him through her improvised hat-turned-eyepiece, she spoke with neither pause nor hesitation, "Trulyanything?YourGraceLordAdmiral? Anything?Doyoureallyhavethewherewithaltotruly answeranything?AnythingImightcaretoask?" Seramis spoke too fast for him to follow.

"Stop! Milady, please. I beg you take hold of your faculties and slow down—"

"Slow? Down?" Lady Seramis repeated, word by word, as if taking control of her voice required her to break her thoughts down into their constituent components. "Your Grace... Henry," she said more familiarly as she took a breath and removed her hat.

Standing up from his writing desk, she spoke in a clear contralto. "Father Time's assault upon reality hasn't slowed, has it?" She crossed to a metal-shuttered window and pushed it open with a loud clang. "It's midday, yet the sun can barely penetrate the gloom. Are we about to face

Ragnarok now that *Fimbulwinter* has descended upon us? Is it not already too late?"

"I'm not sure that I follow you. What do you mean, milady?"

She pointed out the stateroom window. "These clouds mean our end. We may have already lost. Everything we have ever known may be gone within a year or two, and..." Her gray eyes went wide as she spoke. "Henry, if I were to slow down at all, surely I would come to a complete stop."

Closing the shutters as if to shut out the impending devastation, Seramis returned to collapse in the chair. "At least it's already past harvest, so we have that much. But when animals die and crops fail, the people will leave the land and flood the cities. There, the populace will erupt in a violence of despair and desperation. The fall of civilization will be complete and devastating."

"But when the darkness passes, won't there be light? Won't there be a recovery?" Lord Admiral Albion stepped towards her. Seramis turned away, heartbroken at the hope she heard in his voice. She hadn't let herself feel that same possibility.

"Henry, you're thinking about famines brought about by poor harvests, of which there have been plenty in the past hundreds of years. But we're not talking about the loss of an alpine village or a town in northernmost Scandinavia. We're facing the loss of every harvest in Europe and possibly the colonies as well. This is unlike anything we've ever seen."

Henry closed the distance between them. "Then we will need someone like you, with your insights and intelligence, to help us cope with the disaster." A gentle and lopsided smile softened his concerned expression. "And I need you, here, with me. Not buried amidst your studies and your experiments. And I want to be here for you as well. I am truly at your service, Seramis Helleborine."

Softening, Seramis conceded. Her gaze became gentler as she whispered. "Winter is here. But it is not the end. The old myths held that there were two who did, in fact, survive *Fimbulwinter* and *Ragnarok*." Tears welled up in her eyes. "Such loneliness, to be last, to be all alone—"

"If you ever find yourself alone and wish for help, I will be there. I will come for you."

"You just did. Like before. You came for me. You saved me." Lady Seramis spoke in short phrases between sobs.

Taking her hand he knelt before her. "And I shall never forget that gratitude or my relief in providing help."

No sooner had he gone to one knee than Lady Seramis withdrew her hand and stood up in alarm and obvious disquiet. She willed herself to be calm in spite of the anguish pouring through her being.

"Please, Your Grace—" She spoke formally, stifling her sobs and swallowing to counter the rising panic she felt. The candles flickered and only barely dispelled the gloom.

Again he reached for her hand. "What is it?" he asked, still kneeling, consternation creasing his features and hardening his expression.

"I humbly beg you, please stand, Your Grace," Lady Seramis said. Turning away, she spoke with a cool calm. "Your dear friendship has just rescued me again, as I had been truly lost, this time to my own sadness. However, to pursue anything else at this time, when the world itself is fading from sight and the future uncertain..."

Whispered and barely audible, the words slipped from her. "I keep losing everything. My father, my home—"

Albion stood and spoke softly. "Milady, I deeply regret causing you any pain. I only wish to strengthen the bond between us, to explore, together, what it might come to be."

It was evident that he felt empathy for her anguish, and Seramis could tell that he had never let himself completely go into the pure sensual abandon of his affections, not without some stated approval or sign that she felt the same way as he.

"Please, Your Grace," Seramis pleaded, but kept herself turned from him. "I will not forget this great kindness and service you have done me this day, as you are a true friend."

She wondered as she refused to look at him—not trusting to show her true feelings. *How can he accept me as I am? He may think me appealing, but I am no more than a mirage, no more than I allow him to see.*

Albion sounded defeated. "My dear Lady, I will take my leave of you now, taking no small satisfaction that you appear to have recovered—" Obviously saddened, he left the stateroom to nearly collide with Alice just outside the cabin door. After a quick sidestep and a glance back at Lady Seramis, who once again quickly turned away from his gaze, he was into the corridor beyond and swiftly gone.

For the remainder of the voyage back to England, Seramis was truly alone.

In the heart of the United Kingdom, Lady Seramis knelt before her king, addressing her liege from the floor in answer to the first royal question: "Where is my viceroy, the Lord De La Warr?"

Speaking in a loud clear voice, she responded. "He died, Your Majesty, trying to apprehend a traitor that had rebelled against the crown."

Seramis's arrival at court had been a whirlwind of activity. Fortunately, the attendants who normally waited upon the king's sister, Princess Sophie Dorothea, when she was at court were available to assist her. In fact, Seramis hadn't worn cosmetics or a powdered wig since her first night in Virginia Colony many months ago.

Yet old habits remained, as Lady Seramis had once been an instructor of ladies-in-waiting. She now looked and sounded every bit the part of an esteemed noble, easily ingratiating herself at court, becoming an indispensable source of wit and exciting stories—if edited, slightly—from her adventures. But she removed most of those filters now that she was in audience with the king, whose pomp and elegance masked a troubled monarch.

"And who else was part of this rebellion, Dame Commander?" he asked with a soft, slight German accent. Although speaking softly, his voice filled the dark, wood-paneled Great Hall at the heart of St. James Palace. He used the title bestowed upon her in recompense for rescuing the Lady Elizabeth and tracking Patrick Tempus, the fugitive she had just mentioned. Seramis noted that he avoided the use of the title of her noble family—a title that perhaps he still coveted.

"The only other fugitive, Your Majesty, who was a subject to the crown was another commoner named Innes, the one who slew your loyal servant and my patron, Baron Thomas West," she answered, still kneeling. As her legs began to ache, she wondered how long this audience would continue in this manner.

"And what became of him, this—commoner?"

Her near-shout echoed through the oppressive, candle-lit Great Hall, lent weight by her anger and sorrow. "He was slain by Lord De La Warr in the baron's final act of self-defense, sire." Her emotion had not dissipated in the passing of time since the tragedy; the shock was clearly felt amongst the row of councilors that stood behind the throne where King George II held court.

The king drew a deep breath. "The baron will be missed. He has left a void with his passing, and his service to our royal predecessor as well as to us will be noted." Whispering, he addressed one of the councilors who then left the audience, ostensibly for Westminster Abbey, to make preparations for

Lord De La Warr's final resting place according to the quiet instructions Lady Seramis was meant to overhear.

"Your Majesty, the rebellion involved several aboriginal tribes in the colonies—" Lady Seramis was interrupted by a councilor who whispered to the king an audible reminder about the alliances made between England and some of the tribes.

The councilor, in turn, was interrupted by the king. "We can no longer depend upon factionalism and traditional enmity ensuring our supremacy in the colonies." While several councilors noted this and agreed, others began a whispered argument.

"That would be wise, sire." Lady Seramis spoke in a clear voice that silenced the exchange amongst the courtiers. "And I wish to point out that the rebellion attempted to use advanced armaments as our intelligence had indicated. Namely, a fleet consisting of aerial Men-o-War—" Once spoken, her words needed no amplification to cause the councilors to erupt in discussion, until the king raised his gloved hand to silence them.

"You said they *attempted* to use the armaments, Dame Commander?" Incredulity colored his voice and covered his features. "Were they successful?"

"Yes and no, Your Majesty," Lady Seramis said. "When I was abducted, your enemies learned of the compound that was my undoing, the unstable hydrogolic gas that destroyed Helleborine Hall. They attempted to use it—to harness it for its buoyant properties—and their plans to float the aerial men-o-war above cities and armies and rain down destruction would have proved unstoppable but for the gas's susceptibility to a simple spark or open flame." Lady Seramis, for now, left out the part regarding her own airship.

"But the plans from Lisbon didn't mention the compound, did they?" the king asked. She was impressed that the sovereign had looked at the plans, or at least had had someone explain them in the amount of detail needed for him to understand them.

"No, Your Majesty. You are correct that the plans—and indeed, some of the aerial fleet discovered in your Bermuda colony—used heated air for buoyancy. It was the guns and the furnaces from those vessels that led to the destruction of almost their entire fleet."

"Almost?"

"One vessel, their last, was destroyed at the great tower of earth growing out of the island of Bermuda that was itself destroyed, sire. And from that destruction, that enormous volume of dirt now spreads across the skies, blotting out the sun and casting us all into perpetual shadow."

Turning to his councillors, the king gestured towards her. "See, gentlemen? An explanation, at last, for the ill skies."

"Sadly, my liege, I have no explanation for how the column of earth came to be or how it was destroyed." Seramis felt her legs knot into cramps that shot pain from ankles to hips and into her lower back.

Turning back to her, he nodded. "You don't know how many times I've had to listen to countless sermons and predictions concerning the 'end-of-days this' and 'end-of-days that' which were, frankly, beginning to get on my nerves with their lack of specifics."

"Sire, would that this were a divine act. Then, at least, we might gainsay such results by prayer." If lightning were to strike her for her sarcasm, so be it; she would not mince words with him, nor would she pretend to piety. "But without divine intervention as the originator of the calamity I mention, there is no known response that we can muster. As the Duke of Gloucester is my witness, the leader of the rebellion named himself Father Time—"

The king sank in his seat. "*Et tempus omnia vincit...*" His voice trailed off, leaving many to ponder how time conquers all. Although it was the middle of the day, the hall was lit with dozens of candelabras, bright enough to cast shadows of their own.

Protocol be damned. She rose unsteadily, wishing she could massage her aching legs. "—and just as his fleet was vanquished and the rebellion extinguished, he vanished before our eyes." The councilors erupted in a whispered storm, yet a clear contralto carried over them all. "Somehow, he controls or is in league with someone or something that can manipulate elemental forces—"

"*Elementen?*" The king was shocked into speaking German. It was enough to silence the councilors.

Wasn't his first language French?

The king looked directly at Lady Seramis, clearly forgetting his own concerns with protocol and obviously more perturbed by what was described than how it was presented. "Elements like earth? Fire?"

"No, sire. Elemental forces such as described by Sir Isaac Newton: gravity, mass, light... The fundamental properties of elements themselves on an inconceivable scale—"

"Swiftly moving clouds—whether they come from a column of dirt or not—in my experience will as swiftly blow over." The timbre of the king's voice was a practiced and reassuring baritone that filled the hall. "Spring may be delayed, but when it returns—"

"Sire," Lady Seramis interrupted, but none present would repudiate such boldness. "There will be no spring, and after that no summer either. Before it exploded, the column of earth at Bermuda towered out of sight. When it disintegrated, it darkened the sea for thousands of leagues across the Atlantic. To disrupt seasons for the next decade, the storm need only stop one quarter of the sunlight that is blocked at present. Within the next year, Your Majesty, sea water will freeze and one will be able to walk from the Low Countries across the Channel and up the frozen Thames. In five years, ice will cover the North Sea and the North Atlantic to Iceland and beyond. With this cloud cover, snow and ice will accumulate for a century. Under the shadow of the storm, the ice will bury all that we've built. But, long before then, as food runs out and chaos erupts from every quarter, we must prepare for what it means for our civilization to fall!"

"...*Sicut umbra.*" The king's words were barely a whisper.

And to herself, Lady Seramis repeated, "Like a shadow."

Most of all, Father Time feared a repeat of the torture so recently inflicted upon him, as he had never experienced a mix of such misery and pain. But even in the depths of his dread, he had simultaneously admired and loathed the mysterious others claiming to be from the distant future who had ordered him about.

So, I obey their commands, he thought.

By his will alone he diminished in size. But in the quiet sting of his fiery anger at their treatment, he took his time in doing so. The sun quickly rose and rushed across the black sky before setting again, but slower than before. His experience of time actually changed in proportion with his size.

Gravity affects time? Impossible!

Where once the bleak clouds emanating from Bermuda had swiftly drifted past where he could picture his ankles had been, now he found himself standing upon the North American continental shelf on the edge of the Atlantic Ocean. Father Time marched on, dutifully shrinking in size as he strode towards Spanish Florida. His nearly immaterial form only weakly interacted with his environment as the clouds now drifted past the middle of his body.

Astute mortal observers with necessarily long attention spans might discern subtle changes in ocean currents and the movements of clouds as these were the only visible effects of his invisible passage while he traveled miles in mere strides. He noticed the change in his perception of time when he had stood taller than the distance from London to—he guessed—Cambridge. As he diminished, the passing of time, like the passing of the stars across the sky, slowed also, yet his mood and his mania roiled in conflicting thoughts, aims and desires.

"For all my pains, at least I witnessed the end of De La Warr," he said aloud, unheard by any.

At the memory his mood shifted. "That fool Innes had no idea how useful a slave the baron would have been to me. All that training wasted in a failed strike against a girl. What a waste of time that one was!"

At his private joke, fitful laughter that he didn't try to suppress welled up within him. But as he lost control, he guffawed. At the same time, his vision began to skew. Clasping his ghostly hands over his mouth, he chortled and the ground became unstable beneath his feet. With each laugh, his tenuous hold on his immaterial form was undone. He wondered at how his being could be affected by his mirth.

"Do not enjoy yourself overmuch," he said as he willed himself to regain control. "You were never meant to enjoy, rather to destroy."

Stepping upon the shore where the tall trees bent like grasses before him, Father Time thought he recognized the land. It was the area just north of St. Augustine in Spanish Florida, the site of his first military victory. His ethereal chest swelled at the memory of his savage army conquering the fort, slaughtering the soldiers and holding the frightened citizens hostage. He could feel a cruel smirk growing upon his nearly invisible face as he remembered exchanging the lives of the women and children for the fleet that returned to port.

But the vivid memory of the destruction of his once-mighty aerial armada at Bermuda replaced the vision of his personal triumph, The hazy, cloud-covered land before him was overlaid and then eclipsed by the ruined and crushed hulls of his captured fluyts and carracks, smoking and burning in his memory. They had littered the island shoreline where they fell, and his feelings of triumph turned to shame.

"She tricked me into using that damnable, inflammable gas," he croaked, seething at the memory of his loss, blaming once again that Helleborine girl. Striding across fens and waterways, he progressed towards the town of St. Augustine, brooding upon Seramis as he went. "She has been my undoing at every turn!"

By the time he arrived at the farmland on the edge of town, Father Time was a mere twenty feet in height. As the stars vanished, they moved across the sky at a barely noticeable speed, twice what he knew to be customary. A sickly sun rose into a murky gloom to the east, and frost covered the lands wherever Father Time looked. Winter crops had already begun to fail, and the fruit shriveled upon the trees in the frozen mist.

Smoke started to rise from chimneys in the town, as the people struggled with wintry conditions that they were largely unused to. He smiled unnoticed by the few souls who swiftly (as he perceived their meanderings) crossed the town, and at the fishing boats that went to sea in hope of increasing their catch.

Father Time could observe his own form as a faint outline. He continued to diminish as he willed himself to be invisible and stopped at merely ten feet in height. Marveling at the change, he walked amongst the streets of the town, casting an unseen—but evidently felt—pall wherever he went. People crossed themselves in fear and horror as they went about the streets, and he smiled. Yesterday's arrival of the clouds of darkness, or *penumbra de la tristeza*, as he heard them called, had primed them for the anxieties that he stirred with his mere presence.

I have become the perfect spy! His enjoyment was intensely magnified when he arrived at his target: the colonial governor's residence. He simply stepped past the guards and right through the main door as if it were no barrier at all.

Momentarily forgetting his goal, he stepped back and forth through the panels of the closed door. Moving in and out, repeatedly, a broad malevolent grin played upon his face like a small boy teasing his elders. The guards were too disciplined to show it on their faces, but the dread that they felt in the invisible presence of Father Time manifested as knots of tension forming in their shoulders and upper backs and sweat pouring from their features.

Once tired of the novelty, Father Time wondered whether he could be material and immaterial at the same time. In particular, he considered his feet. He pictured them booted, and he stepped and dragged his booted foot against the polished wood. Although he tried to press his foot down through the floor as he had stepped through the solid door, with nothing to push against it was merely as if he shifted his weight from one foot to another.

This felt much different than when he slipped through the closed entrance to the governor's residence. There he would step forward, and his weight would be supported by one leg until he could bring the other down on the same side of the door. Changing his focus from his own body to the material beneath, he visualized the floor as soft clay instead of wood, and he was rewarded with the sensation of his boot sinking slowly into it.

Resting his weight upon one leg, he imagined the same part of the floor to be as yielding as water, and his leg dangled weightless, right through the middle of the boards. Despite his success, he soon tired of his experiments, yet from them felt confident of his adamantine existence.

All around me these pitiful mortals spend their brief lives chasing meaningless pursuits unworthy of the slightest consideration, as I have surpassed them in every way.

It is time to stir things up a bit.

He stood in a hallway directly underneath the governor's office and sensed the portly official sitting at his desk above. Throwing his arms wide and arching his back, Father Time let his head sink forward and remembered the buoyancy he felt when he had first flown in an airship. Slowly, he floated up off the main floor and through the ceiling. He no longer pictured himself wearing the Jesuit habit that was his typical garb, but imagined himself naked. A crown of thorns atop his drooping head and a bloody wound in his side were his only adornments.

"*¡Llorar por mí!*" Father Time cried out for supplication as he manifested in the Governor's office, willing himself visible as he rose out of the floor. "*¡Llorar por mí!*" Of course, even as he cried out, he thought that he shouldn't be mourned by the fat politician in front of him, but worshipped, instead.

But, this should be a good joke, he thought. *And a good way to serve my masters.*

"*¡Dios mío!*" the governor cried in witness to the vision. Crossing himself, the overfed official fell to his knees in prayer.

Father Time resisted the urge to smile, despite being quite satisfied and amused by the sight.

At the man's shouting, Tempus heard footsteps from other officials and more guards outside the office. Instantly, he reached out with his senses, felt the locking mechanisms in the doors, and twisted and melted them solid with a thought. Futile pounding erupted from the hall, interrupting the governor's prayers. Father Time assumed their arrival was the intercession that the fat man had prayed for. Apparently fearful that God had abandoned him, the governor fell back into an unsteady crouch, staring upwards at the floating apparition. "*¡Dios mío!*" he repeated.

"I am your GOD now!" Father Time laughed. Although unlike the earlier episodes there was no distortion to his senses at this jest, he merely felt full of purpose and of malice. He reached down and with one giant hand encircling the governor's throat, proceeded to pull the portly man up to his feet.

Burbling gasps escaped the man's lips as Father Time lifted him, choking, into the air. His hands were still clasped in prayer. Yet Father Time could not have cared less about the sins of this one, and his smile faded. "This is too easy." He dropped the gasping governor onto the floor.

A chill passed through Father Time as he remembered how easily he had been tortured by the others. Brushing the letters and writing instruments aside, Father Time cleared the official's desk and settled his mighty frame atop it.

And in thy best consideration check this hideous rashness, he thought, quoting the Bard as he had done habitually not so long ago.

Crossing his legs, he spoke to the pale man. "You would be better off dead, but why should I be the one to give you some measure of mercy? What have you ever done for me?"

Shaking his head, Father Time sneered at him. "Your predecessor did give me my once-proud fleet... But let's not dwell, shall we?" The promise and potential of world conquest while raining destruction from the skies both saddened him and cheered him.

Looking at the supine form, Father Time noted that the man's color was slowly improving. "I think my original inspiration to terrify you was correct, of course."

The Governor rolled over—groaning in pain—and started to crawl towards the doors.

"Oh no, stay right where you are, Gordo." Lithely, Father Time jumped down from the desk and immaterially inserted his thumb and forefinger into the folds of the back of the governor's thick neck until he came in contact with the spinal cord within the vertebrae. Screams of pain fell silent as Father Time pinched the nerve cluster, sending the man into shock from the pain while simultaneously paralyzing him.

"Interesting," Father Time commented superciliously as the unconscious body fell still. "Almost, but not quite, fascinating—"

"Where was I?" Interrupting himself, he had, without much thought, adopted once again his Jesuit habit, although now suited to and sized for his ten-foot frame. "Oh, yes. Terror, mayhem, general misdeeds." He smiled while the citizens of St. Augustine shuddered around him.

Chapter Three: An Introduction

In which there appears a new aspirant

Lady Seramis gently rubbed her temples with her gloved fingertips, taking care not to touch the wig on her head. Although, if she were to be given free rein, she would indeed push the wig straight off of her head and into a pyre where it could burn and never be missed.

She had been whisked from meeting to meeting with royal councilors and trusted members of Parliament whose functions she could no longer recall and no longer cared to remember. Although her every need had been swiftly and neatly attended to, she was tired, her head hurt, and hunger gnawed indiscriminately at her attention.

The king himself at first was present at many meetings, but it had been seventeen straight hours and she had been questioned by nearly as many officials since she had seen him last. He was supposed to already be here, the Green Drawing Room at Buck House, belonging to Edmund, the Second Duke of Buckingham and Normanby (and only a few years younger than herself, Lady Seramis remembered, having met him and being corrected needlessly upon the difference between County Normanby and the continental region of Normandy), but instead she sat alone, nursing her aching head.

At a knock, Lady Seramis stood and prepared to curtsey, expecting the monarch to walk in surrounded by courtiers, servants, councilors, various nobles and lackeys as could fit into a room this size and not asphyxiate due to the nearly vertical positions of their noses. But it was just one man, alone, who crossed the threshold unannounced and, almost certainly, unwelcome.

In her exhausted state, she nearly returned directly to her seat in disappointment, but she pressed on and observed the forms of etiquette she had recently reacquired upon her return to London. Curtseying, she announced herself, as she had been the only one present, and now, as befitting her station, hosted the newcomer as he closed the doors behind him.

"Good evening! I am the Marchioness de Cambridgeshire, Lady Seramis Helleborine. And you are, good sir?"

"You may call me Voltaire," he said, smiling and bowing before her.

"That's it?" Lady Seramis asked. "Just... Voltaire?" *Could it be?* she thought. *The writer? Jean-Marie... No. François-Marie Arouet?*

"I'm known by many names, mademoiselle." His crooked smile was plain and disarming, and he strode confidently towards the divans and chairs where Lady Seramis stood. *Did he just look up and down my length in bald appraisal?* She realized then that she had done the same to him, and inwardly smiled at the irony.

Flipping open her fan to hide the blend of amusement and annoyance, Lady Seramis said coquettishly, "How many names, monsieur?"

"I try to write them down, but I've lost count of them all. Shall we sit?" He took a place across from her, smoothing his velvet coat and precisely crossing his legs as he sat.

"Please! Are you a writer, monsieur?" Lady Seramis asked, as she, too, sat down gracefully, resting one hand upon the arm of the chair and facing Monsieur Arouet—as she was sure that it was him—directly.

"I am a spy, mademoiselle," Voltaire announced, and added without rancor, "and so are you, of a sort."

"I assure you I am not any profession, monsieur," she corrected, smiling at his directness.

"No, of course not. Nor are you a professional scientist, farmer, or sailor, but as an amateur, you have certainly excelled in all those areas, according to my research. Is that not so, Dame Commander?"

"I'm flattered by being the subject of so exhaustive an examination. And are you a professional spy, monsieur?"

"Well, being a professional writer certainly doesn't pay at present."

"It seems, rather, that it *should* to someone of your talents. I've read some of your poetry, Monsieur Arouet." She placed just the right amount of emphasis on his name.

"Now it is my turn to be flattered. And I will be the first to ask a boon, if you would be so kind as to not repeat that name, which I have left behind long ago."

"*Certainement*," she replied, "and did I also hear rightly of your banishment, which was why you left Paris at the height of your popularity?"

"You are well connected indeed, despite your own banishment." Voltaire looked even more wistful at this. "I mean no offense, as I see yours has been rescinded, where mine is still in effect."

Lady Seramis put down her fan. "We seem to have an equal measure of each other, although I will admit to the superficiality of my understanding. Let me be direct, monsieur. Why are you here? And why do you think me a spy?"

"The answer to both those questions is 'The king ordered it so' and thus, here we are."

Before the conversation could continue, another knock at the drawing room doors brought both spies to their feet to witness the unaccompanied arrival of His Majesty, King George II. He stood in the doorway, while Voltaire bowed and Lady Seramis curtseyed, but didn't wait for them to finish before turning to the servants still in the hall. "Get us some hot food and drink," he barked and then entered the room, while the servants tended to the royal request.

"Damn this drafty house!" the king said as he walked over to the others. Lady Seramis quickly noted that his eyes were red, to match his cheeks. "It takes me forever to warm up when I visit. Who'd want to live here, anyway?" He gestured for the others to sit. "You both are staying at the palace, I presume?"

"Yes, Your Majesty," answered Seramis.

"No, Your Majesty," Voltaire said, turning to look at her as he did so. "I'm staying in the City, at the Old Rectory across from St. Clements." He turned back to the king and was about to continue when, at a knock, the doors opened and in spilled a slew of servants, carrying a table and trays and settings, which were arrayed in the middle of the three, who helped themselves to the king's peculiarly common favorite: braised ox tail, heavy and rich.

"Always in the middle of things, eh, Voltaire?" George II chuckled as he ate some of his dish. The others joined in, with hunger providing the final seasoning. "That's where I need you at present." Pausing, he turned to Lady Seramis. "Cambridgeshire," he said, addressing her by her estate—and surprising her by this confirmation of her family's position. "The crown has a desperate need for you as well." He began, pausing to wash down the ox tail with some hot cider, and revealing why he yielded in the matter of title and property. "The passing of De La Warr has left a void, in more ways than one. He was not only my eyes and ears, but also a very effective lever to apply where diplomacy couldn't reach and war would have been too blunt, if not too costly."

"Your Majesty..." Lady Seramis paused, despite being desperately hungry in addition to being tired, knowing that the rich meal would be difficult to digest. It didn't help that she could picture the late Lord De La Warr, as his death was still a vivid scene before her eyes.

"Let me continue, before you reply." King George held up a bare hand, revealing the near-permanent ink stains resulting from his position. "Voltaire here has both written and demonstrated his support for reason and rational governance but was banished for it by my cousin, Louis. He has been briefed on the calamity we face, but among my peerage, only you and Gloucester have seen firsthand what we're up against." He chuckled a bit. "And I can't send my Lord Admiral to a foreign capital on a mission, can I?" Laughing, he took another draught of cider.

Seramis wasn't sure what the king's aims were. *Does he mean to use the instability to take advantage of the political situation?*

As if reading her thoughts, Voltaire interjected, "The near-perpetual war amongst the so-called civilized countries of Europe must end. Just look at us! A Prussian, a Parisian, and a Virginian!"

"Hanoverian, Voltaire," King George said. "There are no Prussians here."

Seramis would have corrected the writer as well, but remained silent, suppressing her laughter.

"Forgive me, sire. But I beg you allow me to continue my observation as here we are sharing a table in a country estate outside of London, finding common purpose amidst the direst circumstance our kind has yet faced!"

"Yes, well..." The king paused, and continued when no one else spoke. "The English experiment of republicanism in the last century showed that both monarchs and populists have natural limits. But France has never felt that way. And when I say France, I mean Louis. He thinks he is France and France is him. But France is no one thing, as England also is many peoples united. Voltaire mentioned Prussia, and it, too, is a vast collection of diverse people. There are the remnants of the Holy Roman Empire, as well, and the Low Countries! There has only been one thing ever that has united all of us —"

"And that one thing has been when we have been conquered," interrupted Lady Seramis.

"Exactly!" King George exclaimed. "And it could happen again! All of our different little tribes could be swept away under one vanquishing army. And the army we face now could not only defeat our soldiers, but also defeat our agriculture, our culture, and indeed even our civilization." The king had arrived at the business he had wished to address. "I need you both to find out if our adversaries' networks have been infiltrated as Patrick Tempus infiltrated ours. Only you, fair cousin Seramis, have proven their equal, time and again."

He is sincere, Seramis thought. And even if she couldn't discern the royal reason for this request, her curiosity was piqued. But something else awakened within her as well.

"Your Majesty," Lady Seramis replied. "To serve a goal of reason and rational governance, as you put it, you need only but ask, and I am at your command." Seramis formed a thought from a memory from the not-so-distant past, where Europe could become united in purpose while still preserving the diversity of its many traditions. One tradition, however, must needs be addressed.

"I have spoken at length with your advisors, sire," she spoke, and her voice rang out while remaining the same amplitude. "And there is one more thing—in fact, in light of the devastation to our crops it is the most important thing."

"What is it, dear cousin?" the king inquired.

"I cannot very effectively support an institution that condones or allows slavery, my liege." she said.

"Yes, I've been approached by all sides on that very issue," the king answered noncommittally. "If we could do it, a new cultural and economic model, albeit one born of necessity in this crisis, would take time..."

"But it could be done, your Majesty, if you were to take the first step—"

"Do you think me a laggard, dear cousin?" He spoke tersely, but the rancor faded almost immediately. "We've already freed all the slaves that have been bequeathed to this office or somehow came to be in royal possession."

"Your Majesty, it is, of course, an honor and a privilege to see your leadership in action." Seramis remembered the pain and the misery she had witnessed in Virginia. She felt an embarrassment that she had never given a moment's thought to the slaves that she had seen before, but was determined to make up for her blindness of privilege.

"And I concur," Voltaire said, apparently speaking to the king but looking at Seramis with new eyes.

Captain de Ibarra was in a foul mood while piloting the *Agility* into Newport in Virginia Colony. It wasn't the ever-changing winds and weather driving him to distraction. It wasn't the anxieties of leaving his friend and the owner of his vessel in the company of the English, who had previously banished her (and could do much worse, as he knew). No, it was the way this vessel now handled itself when sailing. It may be *The Agility of Clouds* when in flight, but it was the *'tucas de macaco* when on the water.

It also didn't help to think of his brother, but he had a captive audience in White Apple, and her fascination didn't prevent her from asking questions.

She had descended from her station the crow's nest as the captain attempted to make the berth in port. "What's a privateer?" She asked, without rancor but apparently without being aware of the personal and political implications of the question.

"Prepare to haul about! Again!" Captain de Ibarra shouted, ignoring the question. Even the gloomy sky hiding a weak winter sun would be worth noting if this top-heavy craft would just bite its keel into the current a little. But when the ship sailed like a rudderless barge everything was grey and glum to the captain, so it mattered little what the actual sky looked like.

"I said, what's a—"

"I heard you," the captain said tersely. "But I haven't got all day to stand here and explain—"

"You said you and your brother were both captains. How can you both be captain?" White Apple interrupted. Her eyes were wide with interest.

"On different ships, my dear," he said with a sigh. "Before I commanded this lumbering vessel, my brother and I both captained caravels."

"Like this one?"

"No, they were larger and square-sailed, almost like a galleon..." the captain's voice trailed off.

"What happened with the galleon?"

"What? How did you—" the captain sputtered the words. "Shouldn't you be getting ready to go ashore?"

Hanaawa called out to White Apple from the main deck, "I'm going to leave you in the captain's charge while I go to the McClures' at New Helleborine Hall, so show a little respect!"

"I'll remember you said little," White Apple shouted back.

The captain cried out as the realization dawned slowly upon him. "You're going to what?"

Hanaawa walked back to the wheel deck. "Oh, sorry. I should have mentioned it sooner," he said to the captain and cocked his head at the Spaniard's fierce expression. "Unless you want to go to the McClures and break the news that Lady Seramis is—"

"Uh, no," replied Captain de Ibarra. "But your niece? Isn't she a lady-in-waiting? Isn't she supposed to stay at the hall and—I don't know—wait?"

"Well, not that I know of," Hanaawa said. "And it seems that there are a number of improvements she wants to make to the *Agility*..."

"She what?" bellowed the captain.

"Didn't she mention any of that to you?"

"You're in league with her," the captain accused. "The damn ship flounders like a lovesick sea-cow, and I'm supposed to let some landlubber experiment on—"

"Not without your approval, of course," she said innocently, looking every inch a pleading waif, merely wanting to help. "Maybe after all this we can find out whatever happened to your brother's ship?"

"Don't distract me! Aren't you supposed to be at your post?"

He would have continued the argument but he managed the berth at last. White Apple's questions had touched a nerve. Without the feeling of satisfaction he usually felt, he notified the crew that they had arrived at their destination, enacting the standing orders upon making landfall.

Hanaawa arrived at New Helleborine Hall, but instead of the colonist household he had found when fleeing the fiery-eyed demon Father Time, it had grown into an outpost of commerce and trade in the center of Virginia Colony. Despite the low clouds darkening the land, he marveled at the tumult of construction and din of activity, the braying of farm animals and the shouting of workers. *Is this the future of this land?*

The weak crepuscular light was fading fast. Countering the gloom and welcoming the traveler, the kitchen aromas, the boisterous talk, and the convivial laughter warmed him. *It is a future that honors the past. It could be a good model for any who wished to follow.*

Colonel McClure, the majordomo of New Helleborine Hall and Seramis Helleborine's trusted advisor, greeted him upon his arrival. "I've only met you twice—and this is the first time we're both not wounded—but I'd recognize you in an instant, Hanaawa! Come in, you're just in time for some supper!" His hearty voice was warm and kind, but his eyes were sharp and his jaw set. Both wore soft buckskin and would have almost appeared identical in dress except for the beadwork and fringe on Hanaawa's attire.

Hanaawa relaxed at the invitation. "Thank you, Colonel. I'd guess your role here by your bearing even if I didn't recognize you. I'll just wash away this grime from the road, if you can point me in the direction where to do so!" Patting the dust from his leather breeches, he looked around the compound at the many buildings and the large barn, where his nephew had passed away, not so long ago but seemingly in a different age than present.

"That would be inside, McClure said, his smile growing. "We've added indoor plumbing here since your last visit." He gestured towards the lit parlor within his modest home, the first house built here, if Hanaawa remembered correctly from his brief stay.

Once inside, Hanaawa was greeted warmly by Mrs. McClure. But the mood shifted with the news that Dame Seramis, the mistress of the hall, was on her way back to England. When the situation was explained, it was greeted with stoic acceptance by both McClures despite the remarkable events he conveyed. They talked through the entire evening meal, with Hanaawa sharing in equal parts his own tale of the adventures upon the sea and in the sky and the disaster that had descended upon them all.

Mrs. McClure's descriptions of life here in Virginia Colony were an equal mix of progress heralding a bright possible future and dark forebodings since the arrival of the never-ending gloom. Hanaawa shared her concerns, and repeated how grateful he was for her ministrations when he had been wounded and for her hospitality in the present.

"I don't know whether to feel relief," Mrs. McClure said, "knowing there's an actual source to this gloom or to feel fear that someone can wield as much power as you say. How can we hope to stop such a monstrosity?" Her husband patted her arm in empathy. She smiled as she continued, "But there is hope if we have an ally like the mistress—now a commander, you say? If anyone could defeat such a thing, it would be the one who could make a ship sail through the air!"

Brightening, Hanaawa agreed. "It's incredible, and I hope you see the 'airship' soon—but more than just her accomplishments, I hope you get to see her take charge. Lady Seramis is the bright side of a coin, the opposite side of that Father Time creature. She brings together and inspires where he merely destroys."

"Aye," Colonel McClure agreed. "But who can possibly be the equal of someone or something called Father Time? There is more at play here, far beyond anything I've experienced. Some pieces on the board that we can't see..."

"...Or players of the game we can't comprehend!" Hanaawa agreed.

"That much is clear, gentlemen," Mrs. McClure interjected. "Moses didn't part the Red Sea all by himself, did he? And you say this Father Time stopped a hurricane in place? Did you not also mention how he spoke of vast powers?"

"I don't know if I have the telling of it, ma'am." Hanaawa's voice became distant. "But you're right. And there must be a reason why our Lady Seramis is as she is as well." His eyes sought a horizon that only he could see. "There's something that intertwines the two, but I can't see what it is—"

"That's because you're tired." The colonel looked a little nervous as he ended the discussion. "Get some rest, and we'll have a reconnoiter in the morning. I'll help you take in the lay of the land."

That night, as he slept, Hanaawa walked among nightmares and dreamscapes of uncountable horrors.

The Fury of Storms

Detached and unemotional, he merely stepped from scene to scene as his own memories were twisted and arrayed in terrifying visions. Amidst fire and smoke, his people, the Natchez, ran from their homes while he watched. Shouts and cries of anguish split the air before being drowned out by the constant roar of the flames that engulfed their homes. Warriors with four arms—towering twice the height of his kin—ran amongst the faltering defenders, slaying all they could reach. And yet, they ignored the war chief Hanaawa who stood in the midst of the carnage, passive and motionless.

Only Hanaawa's labored breathing and clenched fists betrayed his inner turmoil as he sought a calm to balance the bloodshed he witnessed. Once his kin had all been slain, Natchez he had never seen before—antecedents from a bygone age—approached him and pleaded for their lives, begging Hanaawa to take action and fight back. The four-armed warriors rushed directly to Hanaawa, where he could see their skin peeled back from their faces revealing bloody and lidless eyes. They smiled death-like grins with mouths that had no lips. Mercilessly, they slew the innocents pleading to Hanaawa for succor—or failing that, begging for bloody vengeance.

Unmoving in his lucid dream, unlike his actual body flailing and twisting upon the cot laid out for him in the parlor, Hanaawa ignored the demons and tried to open his perception to the dream movements and shapes beyond his nightmare. Despite the carnage that surrounded his dreaming self, he willed himself to calm. The enraged horde then fell directly upon Hanaawa himself, rending his clothes, tearing at his flesh, pulling his limbs from his body.

He felt a spear enter his eye socket in horrible burning pain, but Hanaawa took a deep breath and let a benign inner light flood his being. A ragged knife ripped at his throat, but Hanaawa imagined a pool, serene and sweet, into which he fell away from his dream body. While beads of sweat condensed upon his sleeping body in the cold night air where he had twisted away from his nightclothes, Hanaawa floated serene and bodiless through the nightscape of his dream.

"You have taken everything from me," Hanaawa said in his dream. "Why do you hide? Why do you still fear me?" His words grew and took the form of a tree unlike any that had ever been seen. Six large branches grew low upon the smooth trunk, and curved upwards, sleek and shiny. From these large branches, all the smaller branches grew vertically in straight lines at equal distance from the other, each terminating at the same height as the rest. And from each tip, a single leaf, ovoid in shape, glowed with an intense luminosity wherever dreamlight touched its surface. The tree silently called out all within the dream; its light sought to reveal any who inhabited the realms of slumber.

"You are out there, are you not?" Hanaawa asked, feeling a presence revealed by the newly formed tree and his questing senses. "You have the ability to enter dreams, all dreams, any and every dream. You see me as I am, yet you cower in shame and fear. Why is that?" Waving, undulating mosses writhed about the trunk of the mystical tree before spreading in all directions. Tiny sprouts appeared in places where Hanaawa's soul had been touched. Some tangled, some shot upwards; many grew and then withered, returning to the moss to be joined with the rest before sprouting again.

"I have not the sense of shame you think." Distant words floated upon the currents of Hanaawa's dreams, echoing and susurrating in a sibilant stream of hatred and contempt. Like poisonous wisps, the words whipped through the dream air, curling about themselves and lashing out in equal measure. "I have not the thought of fear and yet—from you alone, upon the brink, a sense of desperation do I get!" In rhythmic pulses, the words pounded upon the tree from every direction. In sympathetic vibration, the tree joined and then amplified the meter, turning the pulse upon the unseen speaker.

Sensing his opening, Hanaawa's enchantment began.

> *"Let he who would the world rule,*
> *Speak out of pride but sound a fool,*
> *Reveal the master, of whom he fears,*
> *Repent his folly in bitter tears!"*

With each metric accent, the words flowed and throbbed through the tree and throughout the dream until soon they surrounded a smoky shape not unlike a man, who twisted and turned in the trap of the spell.

Shrieking and moaning, the shape spoke in a rage that burned out of control.

> *"Aye, the others you shall someday see*
> *Have true power that can forever be."*

The words poured forth, even as the shape tried to pull them back.

"But know your folly will avail you little,
And you shall soon choke upon my spittle!"

With a snap, the shape vanished before coalescing into a recognizable form.

Gasping, Hanaawa woke. "That was a horrible rhyme!"

Chapter Four: An Indiscretion

In which love and hate are not what they seem

Lady Seramis fell asleep immediately upon settling into bed that night as it was the first time she had rested in a bed on solid ground in months. She woke several times through the night, but fell back to sleep quickly each time; the feeling of unease passed, forgotten in slumber. Upon waking into a dim gray morning, she sat up and took in the details of Queen Anne's bedroom in St. James's Palace, still preserved in its original form. She studied the textures, the dark colors of the wood, and lost herself in her observations as she hadn't in months, if not years.

However, she soon remembered that the last time she had been idle like this upon waking was on the day of the party hosted by the late Lord De La Warr, the day of the accident that had nearly burned the original Helleborine Hall to the ground. For a moment, Lady Seramis wished she could just sink deeper into the bedding and lose herself, forgetting all that had happened and ignoring all that was about to happen.

As soon as she completed her morning ablutions and was about to ring for breakfast, a palace servant announced that a gentleman caller had arrived and was currently waiting downstairs. Thinking warmly of him who she wished to see, Lady Seramis inquired if he could join her for her meal, but heard that he had already requested to host her in the drawing room facing the southern courtyard, and that she could join him whenever she wished.

Maids quickly dressed her as befitting the expectations of her station, and she personally added the ribboned sash and medallion from her order. The servants complimented her upon her comportment, but she couldn't shake the feeling that she was on display. In her gown, she felt she was an object meant to be observed instead of an agent of her own volition. This troubled her for the first time in her young life. But rather than reinvent herself while her gentleman caller waited below, she merely dispensed with the powder and face paint that were currently fashionable. The periwig lay untouched, having never even been considered.

Arriving downstairs at the day room, Dame Seramis fully expected to be reunited with Lord Admiral Henry Albion, Duke of Gloucester, but was greeted instead by Voltaire, who had returned to Westminster from the City.

"Somewhere, a principality is quite evidently missing its princess," Voltaire said in greeting, bowing deeply.

"Monsieur, umm... I'm sorry, I was expecting someone else." It took her but a moment to collect herself and adjust her thoughts, more distracted by the disappointment of missed expectations than the condescending flattery. "Good morrow to you. It hardly seems a moment since we last met."

Voltaire plucked at his lace cuff so he need not look her in the eye, clearly disappointed in her reaction. "I apologize as well, mademoiselle, and if I could be him who you were anticipating, I would be the happier for it." He turned to a pair of heavy salon chairs set about a table covered with a fine damask cloth. "I wanted to thank you for your improvised graciousness when you welcomed me last night. I would like to return the honor. Please join me, and perhaps we can talk over some breakfast."

"It was nothing but a polite response, monsieur, and you are most welcome." Seramis curtsied and took her seat. Hot water was brought in, but she declined tea. Her companion's composure having returned, he smiled across the table. A ribbon tied the long thick hair that framed his expressive face. Lady Seramis pretended not to look so closely as she deftly applied some apple preserves to thinly sliced bread.

Voltaire helped himself to some cheese and launched into conversation. "I continue to be most impressed, mademoiselle, by one possessed of such strength of character to impose upon even a monarch a moral standard of virtue."

"Monsieur, please don't think me churlish or dismissive." Lady Seramis found his flattery out of character, at least according to what she knew of him from her reading. "As His Majesty pointed out, he had already acted according to his own virtue. I was merely voicing an echo of what had previously been decided."

Sitting back in his chair, Voltaire shook his head. "I have tried to imagine many things, but I wouldn't think you dismissive unless you had just cause. I can also gather from the flow of our conversation that you are not to be charmed into being receptive."

"Is that, monsieur, what you are trying to accomplish?" Her tone was gentle yet pointed, the forward nature of his comment having taken her by surprise.

He leaned forward. "Of course! What is polite discourse but an attempt to smooth over the rough edges of our needs and desires? To make palatable the differences in temperaments and tastes that multiply and are magnified by differences in upbringing and history? What else would allow us to converse, milady?"

"I disagree, monsieur," she said with a smile. "You mean to state that this conversation—or any—wouldn't be possible without conventions of society? If that is your premise, I think it would be easy to disprove."

As he formulated his response, she noticed a certain smugness at the corners of his eyes and lips.

"If I could refine that proposition, mademoiselle—in that, if we had nothing in common, or were in fact at cross purposes in our desires, milady, we could still follow the forms of protocol and pleasantly share this lovely conversation and breakfast."

At the mention of the word 'desires' Lady Seramis thought again of the person she'd originally hoped to share her breakfast with. A picture of the duke of Gloucester, in all his martial bearing and reserve, briefly played about her vision.

"See?" Voltaire asked, interrupting her reverie.

"I beg your pardon." Slightly flustered, she smoothed her skirts and fixed her focus once more upon Voltaire.

"Just now, you left this conversation—" he said.

"I most certainly did not..." she snapped, before her voice trailed away with a guilty flash she felt but hoped didn't show.

In the silence that followed, the two looked closely at one another. A charming half-smile still played about Voltaire's face as he regarded Seramis, who relaxed.

"Indeed, monsieur," she sighed. "At that moment I was in fact thinking of someone else, someone who is a very good friend to me." But the thought of Henry upon his knee belied the casualness of her words, and she stopped before continuing to describe him, or the friendship she felt—if that were truly all that she felt.

"And I don't mean to repeat myself, milady, but without common cause or common courtesy, our cross purposes would be an impediment to our conversation."

"But we do have common cause," she insisted. "We serve the king and must save our culture and preserve our civilization. Further, as advocates of reason and rationality, our methods as well as our aims are in comity, reciprocal and inclusive—"

"But I think our desires aren't yet mutual, Dame Commander Seramis Helleborine," Voltaire said as he leaned forward in his chair. "For I desire you as I have never felt and—despite trying—never imagined that I could desire anyone!"

Seramis laughed. "Oh, monsieur, you speak of protocols, but then vouchsafe such improprieties!"

"Did I not say that the protocols smoothed over uncouth roughness?"

"Yes, indeed. But am I so newly arrived here at court that I missed the fashion of forwardness?" Seramis put down her cider, sitting back in her chair.

"The protocols remain unchanged, and I am sadly out of fashion at present." Voltaire crossed his arms, his head leaning back slightly. "Although in general, our circumstances are indeed altered. I seek now to speak plainly, if you wish."

"I thought at first you intended to charm me to being receptive," Lady Seramis rejoined.

"Which failed, as we both noted. So I spoke my feelings plainly, which apparently also failed to impress upon you the sincerity of my desires. Might I add, you've not even asked what my desires are."

"Monsieur, you're French. I think we both know—"

"Please don't presume, milady—"

"But I do presume to know my own mind! And I know that there are some things best left unsaid—"

"Of course, and you are correct in presuming the reciprocal comity of our reason and rationality. But, milady, all I'm proposing is a partnership—"

And at that, time slowed even more for Seramis, whose patience had been strained near to its limits by the discussion. As she listened, she found that she could withstand better the declarations of emotions that she had once experienced as excruciating, but which were now demoted to extremely intense.

She thought about how the passion she experienced speaking with Voltaire differed from her experience with the duke. With a smile, she interrupted him. "Monsieur, no proposals, please. They're not necessary. We are partners in a task assigned by His Majesty, the king." Leaning forward, she confided, "And if our present situation were not so dire, I assure you that a similar proposal from another would have already been received and, indeed, most certainly welcomed."

Outside St. James's Palace, the scene was very different as snow continued to fall, and the morning light yielded nothing more than a shadowy gloom. Londoners were already withdrawing from the streets, their day over before it even began, forced back indoors by the frigid cold. The markets would soon be empty, the streets almost deserted. From poor peddler to wealthy merchant, all were affected by the near total cessation of trade and activity, although the poor, naturally, bore the brunt of it and were first to suffer.

Deprivation was commonplace amongst the poor, but even the sources of alms—the churches—were empty as the storms made travel deadly for many, even in the heart of the capital. Like the sun, the spirit of the City faded and retreated into perpetual twilight. Even in the few places where people gathered, the air fairly reeked of desperation, and the few shouts and peals of forced laughter were subdued under the onrushing blanket of snow.

The thickest blanket of floating particulates seemed to hover in the sky over Northern Europe, from Normandy and the Low Countries to Scotland, and from Ireland to Sweden. The global air currents had pushed the shroud that grew from the devastated tower of earth at Bermuda as far as the Mediterranean and the Balkans. Nearly all inhabitants within the numerous cities of the vast region were laid low, but some few still thrived as gloom inspired the devout—or the seemingly devout—to exhort their fellow sufferers to repent at what was surely the end of days.

Not yet suffering the constant snowfall that forced travelers off the roads in the North, the people of the Mediterranean communed in the stygian days where they could, either in devotion or revels. The aristocracy invented new fashions and new games and distracted themselves from the fading light that dimmed each day. Those who toiled in service to their masters tried, in turn, to ignore the toll of forced jollity and practiced cheer, working in increasing silence.

And out of the silence that surrounded the noisy cities, something unusual arose. The outsiders and the solitary ones, the castaways and the disinherited all stirred, as if moved by unseen forces. Shadowy figures now wandered in shadowy days. Those groups that lived outside of civil society, away from the cities bound by networks of roads, some who had long ago grouped themselves by names such as Roma or Gypsy, banded together out of a vague sense of unease and restlessness—or possibly opportunity.

The lonely guard posts of civilization grew more isolated. Some were even abandoned in the face of the newly aroused, uncounted rabble. Outposts on the frontiers became islands within a sea of faithlessness without allegiances, where good folk huddled out of fear of the surging outcasts that no longer slipped away quietly when opposed.

Along lines of ancient power, to be someday mapped by far-future psychic cartographers, the dispossessed moved. Still scattered and fragmented, but now oriented and directed, they traveled with new purpose. But—whether they went like farm animals to the slaughter or like spiders attracted by vibrations within their web was yet to be seen.

C.J. Pitchford

Captain de Ibarra was still frustrated, but what was a distraction earlier was now the source of his ire.

"What happened to your brother?" White Apple laid the plans she had created upon the captain's desk. Her questions hadn't ceased, except during sleep, and the return of the wan daylight brought a return of her curiosity—a curiosity the captain found too painful to bear.

"Why do you keep bringing that up?" He asked, but noting her pained expression, continued without waiting for an answer. "His life ended in a violent folly, a volley, to be sure—"

"What?" White Apple removed her ink-spotted apron and folded it upon her lap, signaling every intention of staying.

Captain de Ibarra sighed and pushed himself back further into his seat, away from his desk. "The only time I've ever seen anything like it—his ship was blown into pieces by a Spanish galleon—"

"How?"

"Oh, she was beautiful—an irresistible siren, heavy with gold—sitting so low in the water as to be little more than spars, masts and sails," the captain closed his eyes and pinched the bridge of his aquiline nose. "My brother never faltered, even when all its guns were brought to bear. I was right behind him, cursing him for a fool even as I attempted to be the greater fool who follows a fool."

"Very foolish."

"Indeed." His eyes opened with a pained expression. "The ship vaporized right in front of me when caught in the line of fire. And I was sailing so closely behind him—in a ship identical to its twin in every respect—it must have appeared to the Spanish gunners that the cannonshot had no effect. I sailed right through the cloud of debris that was all that was left of him and his ship. Yet, as the cannons hesitated in their confusion, it gave me a chance to escape."

"But why did your brother attack a heavily armed vessel?"

"I don't know. Maybe he hoped to be rich beyond measure. Maybe he sacrificed himself to try to ensure my safety. But in any case, even when facing certain death, one holds true to one's course. That's just how he was."

"And how you are, as well?" White Apple put a gentle hand upon his arm.

"Not everything works out as one intends." He turned to the plans she had drawn, admiring their potential. "However, this might work!" he said slowly, while holding a lantern over the drawings and studying every detail no matter how minute.

"Might work?" White Apple asked incredulously. "The calculations of the force differentials predict improvements at least fifty-fold over the aerialwave." She spoke emphatically, but without pride.

"And I get my gun ports back!" No one could mutter like the captain, and she cocked her head to hear him better.

"What was that?"

"Nothing," he said quickly. "Why do you have three of these—what are they? These things that look like scimitars?"

"Those are the blades that push the air, and thus propel the airship through the sky." She pointed to the main drawing. "I call the assembly a propellant, as its rotation allows the blades to cut into the air. My calculations show that three equiangular blades provide the right mix of momentum and balance while turning."

"It all seems so easy, so natural," the captain remarked, "almost like a toy—I meant no disrespect."

"As it turns out, you're right." Her dark eyes gleamed in the light of the lantern.

"What?" he shouted, setting down the lantern with a clang. "This ship is no toy! Do you mean to be playing about with it?"

"I meant no disrespect, either, señor," White Apple said as she gently handed the captain a small, dried seed pod. "Here's the toy that inspired me..."

He laid it in his palm and peered at it. "What's this?"

"Well, obviously, it's a seed."

"I know that! Why did you give it to me?"

"Hold it up," she instructed. "Now, gently let it fall."

As he tilted his weathered hand the seed slid from it, but when it caught the air it began to twist and spin, thus slowing its descent.

White Apple whispered, "We used to play with these, my brother and I..."

The catch in White Apple's voice when she mentioned her brother drew the captain's attention away from the seed. The youth had died on Lady Seramis's lands in Virginia. Glancing across at her, he noted her quivering lip and shaking shoulders. For all her genius and quirks of perception, she was still just a girl, wearing simple homespun clothes made in the colonies.

He gave her a quiet moment to recover. Straightening, the captain cleared his throat and spoke a bit too loudly. "Well! What are you going to do with these plans? Frame them?"

"What?" White Apple was in shock.

"Or would you rather buy the parts, hire the smithies and ironmongers and build them?" Captain de Ibarra fairly shouted, white teeth flashing in the lamplight. Drawing a bag of coins from his pocket and spilling them on the desk, he brushed them with the flat of his hand. They flowed across the plans like a tiny golden stream.

Her eyes narrowed. "Where did you get those?"

"From the wreck of the scuttled frigate before we left Bermuda, of course."

"You stole them?" One brow lifted in appreciation.

"Did not!" His pride ached. "Spoils of war, missy. Spoils of war." Scooping them up, he grumbled, "I need to buy the materials to properly replace the rudder we improvised down on the sandy coast. And here I thought I'd offer you a chance to see your invention made real. I would have wagered it would have only taken you—oh, no more than a week to have it all built and set aboard. After all, Lady Seramis gave you her notes and asked you to take a look..."

"That was for safekeeping!"

"And you've been keeping them safe." He barely paused to nod to her. "And you could keep us all that much safer, if you could improve on the aerialwave by fifty-some differences of force things! But no, you have to get all high and mighty—"

"I am not," she protested.

"Prove it."

"You just reminded me that if I had four of these," White Apple said, pointing to the propellants she designed, "I could implement my aerial rudder plan. I hope you didn't get too attached to those blood coins. We have work to do. Come on!"

Chapter Five: A Situation

In which conflict and spying are merely symptomatic

The journey from London to Paris was laborious and slow due to the harsh weather, but Dame Seramis and Voltaire made good use of the time by rehearsing their new roles as they bounced and jolted over the frozen roads, trying not to think of what would befall them should a wheel be thrown or an axle broken. It had been simple to decide upon a course of action, but making the plan work would take both considerable practice and good fortune. They merely had to ascertain whether or not war would break out in Europe, and then, put a stop to it, of course.

Both were heavily bundled against the elements, accompanied in the coach by two of their four drivers, who doubled as men-at-arms. Like the horses in the train that pulled the coach, the coachman and the postilion driving the lead horse were rotated frequently, as none could directly face the frigid winds for more than a few hours. The two in the compartment studiously paid no attention to Seramis and Voltaire as the spies spoke tirelessly about their plans and practiced the assumed identities that matched their letters of introduction and other documents.

They had only just arrived in Normandy after being ferried across the icy English Channel and were setting out on their route south toward Paris when they came upon a small group of pikemen blocking their way. The driver leapt down from his seat, brandishing a musket. Just as the wheels ceased crunching on snow, the other men-at-arms threw open the doors and jumped out to join him. Voltaire leaned towards the open door as a pretext to see better when he called out in English, "What is it? Why are we stopped? I was told that we would present ourselves in Desvres, not here in some forsaken forest!"

"You are *Anglais*?" A sergeant swathed in furs stepped forward to inspect the interior of the coach and accepted a copy of the traveling papers from one of the drivers. He looked them over studiously, not allowing his illiteracy to prevent him from reading them.

"Of course!" shouted Voltaire. He pretended to be slightly drunk, letting his grip on the coach door slip from time to time. His role was that of a merchant identified in the traveling papers as Sir Thomas Cheltenham.

"Apologies, monsieur. We have not so many of the travelers these days." The sergeant replied, handing back the papers that threatened to follow the gusts of winds into the woods beyond the road.

"Just as well," Voltaire conceded. "Time to thaw out some frozen drivers, anyway. Hey! You up front there. Do you need an invitation?" At this, the postilion descended from the near lead horse, while his position was taken up by one of the men who had just gotten out, trading his gun for the heavy iron boot covers worn when in the saddle.

From behind Voltaire, a silky voice purred in between exaggerated shivering, "*Dieux bons, qu'il fait froid!*"

Surprised, the sergeant lost what little English he had. "*Qui est-elle?*"

And as Voltaire leaned back in his seat, all the French soldiers outside leaned in to peer at Dame Seramis, transformed by face paint and a curled wig into an unrivaled beauty, equal parts noblewoman and courtesan. Pouting coquettishly, she played her part as she enchanted the squad.

"This, of course, is my companion, the Mademoiselle Dunoyer," Voltaire said. Turning back to them, he exclaimed, "Ye must be starved." His accent was a mix of Cornwall and Devon, a soft Southwest England drawl emphasized by the cheese he was eating. "Have you tried this?" He offered the French soldiers a wheel of cheese. "It's cheddar, of course, infused with horseradish."

The soldiers looked hungrily at the food and at each other, but had the discipline to wait to move forward.

"Here, take it. I've got another and if I eat too much of it... Well, I stop right up." Voltaire spoke with a practiced familiarity. The dim light of day pierced the darkened coach just enough to highlight Lady Seramis's beautiful features as she leaned back in the seat, rolled her eyes, and crossed her arms.

"Well, good sirs?" Voltaire asked of the soldiers. "Are we going to just stay out here for the rest of the available light?" One of them stepped forward at a gesture and took the cheese.

"*Non, monsieur. Bonne chance.*" The sergeant wished them luck, but appeared uneasy. The new men took their positions; those who had just been relieved entered the coach and closed the door behind them. Cracking his whip, the driver shouted a loud "Hyah," and they resumed their journey, slowly leaving the soldiers behind.

"Beg pardon, I wonder why they stopped?" the newly relieved coachman said, looking around at the others within the coach.

"What do you mean, sir?" Seramis dispensed with her affected role as they continued traveling. "Why did they stop us in the middle of the road?"

"No, milady. I wonder why they stopped robbing us? I mean, it's not easy to hide a leveled crossbow. Even when you stand behind a tree next to the road..."

"So that explains the stop in the middle of the woods," Voltaire said.

"But why did they let us go?" Seramis asked.

"Begging your pardon, milady." The driver who had recently ridden postilion spoke up. "But I think they were starving, not thieves."

"And I think they appreciated your beauty, milady," Voltaire said.

Turning to him, she asked, "I thought it was cliché that all Frenchmen were susceptible to a powdered face and pursed lips? And cheese?"

"*C'est possible*?" Voltaire smiled. "But be glad we aren't yet in Paris. Once there, nothing will stop the men from chasing you incessantly!"

Seramis and Voltaire arrived at the gates of Paris after days of travel and sat in their coach in the cold. The city was closed. They waited along with an ever-growing host of travelers similarly interrupted amidst the growing towns that surrounded the walls of the city. The gates were closed, the chains within the Seine hauled up and pulled taut, and none were allowed to enter or leave the city. All who arrived were advised to return home, but few did so. A line of coaches soon littered the sides of the fortified *Redoute* outside La Chapelle leading to one of the many gates.

"It appears that we won't be arriving in Paris in the style to which we've become accustomed," Voltaire commented wryly, looking through the tiny window in the coach door. "Like us, the snow would appear to have stopped as well, so there is that, at least."

"The line for entrance to the city has grown behind us, preventing us from leaving as well as entering," Seramis said. "We have to come up with another plan."

"Do we?" Voltaire asked nonchalantly. "Certainly, our timetable is not adversely affected by this delay?"

"*Certainement*, monsieur," Dame Seramis reached into the space between the seat cushions upon which she sat and the walls of the coach. "But why take that chance?"

From a side compartment she lifted a case containing several smaller cases and with a mirror upon the inside of the lid. "Pardon me, gentlemen," she said to the rest of the traveling party, "but I require a moment."

Pulling on a brace along the ceiling of the coach, Lady Seramis revealed a slot in the material. After digging slightly into the gap she created, she pulled a hidden cord down from the ceiling, where one end had been fastened. She then threaded it through three hooks on the right side of her case before securing the cord back at the ceiling. Repeating the process on the left with a similar cord, she soon had her case secured in front of her like a suspended vanity.

With her hands now free, she quickly removed the pins from her wig and bound her hair more tightly with a dark band. Her fingers flew among the inner cases in search of the cold cream that was needed to remove her face paint and rouge. She then applied a dark gray base from her forehead all the way down to her décolletage.

Voltaire stared openly as she closed her case, replaced the cords in the ceiling, and set the kit back into its hiding space.

He was caught in the act when she held out her wig to him.

"What?" he said, missing what he had just been asked.

"I said, would you be so kind as to hold this?" Seramis repeated.

"*D'accord*, mademoiselle," he managed to squeak as he took the wig.

"Gentlemen," Lady Seramis began, addressing the drivers who feigned sleep. "Could you shift just a bit away from where I sit? Please point your knees at Sir Thomas, here. I require but a bit more space from you both."

As soon as they complied, she rose from her seat and shifted ninety degrees, although she couldn't stand up completely. Lifting the seat with one hand, she held out the other for her wig. When Voltaire gave it back to her, she placed it upon a bust within a compartment under the seat, meant to keep the shape of the wig when not in use. Pulling the bewigged bust towards the front of the compartment, she reached farther in and pulled out a box that she then placed upon the seat once it was again closed.

"This is the difficult part," Lady Seramis said to no one in particular, but knowing that in the tight quarters, she might as well be addressing them all.

She noted that Voltaire, having apparently come to his senses, and made quite the display of not looking directly at her. "Women," he said. "Why does changing one's attire require such—"

"Monsieur?" Seramis interrupted, wishing to continue her preparations as quickly as possible. Her legs were beginning to cramp, and the strain of hunching over was beginning to knot the muscles along her back.

She crossed her arms at her waist. Taking handfuls of her traveling gowns, she pulled all of them over her head in a single motion, revealing dark hose and a long-sleeved top.

These were garments she had made upon the model of the outfit—originally a puppeteer's hose and costume—she had worn while spying in Lisbon. But whereas that had been made of silk and cloth, she now wore dark leather for protection against the elements.

Seramis handed her clothes to Voltaire. Wordlessly, he took them. She then opened the box, taking out leather-padded black slippers which she dropped onto the floor in front of her, a dark cap which she placed upon her head, and a pair of gloves which she donned, rendering her completely in dark grays and black from head to toe.

"I'll take that now," she said, folding the gowns and placing it on the seat. She then set the closed box upon the clothes. "I shan't be gone long. It's too cold to move slowly."

"What?" Voltaire asked. Seramis slid her feet into the slippers, reached behind her to unlatch the coach door, and bumped it open with her derriere. With a broad wink to him and nods to the rest, she said, "Thank you, gentlemen, for your patient attendance. I pray you continue to be patient until I return." With that she turned and hopped out without looking back.

With a look of astonishment upon his face that bordered upon the comical, Voltaire slowly pulled the door closed and latched it.

Hours passed. Arguing travelers came and went outside the coach. Some even tried to get arrested on purpose in order to gain admittance to the city. They were simply abused for their pains and pushed bodily even farther down the road away from the entrance. The tumult eventually died away, as more snow began to fall.

Just as Voltaire's concern for Dame Seramis's unusual and unplanned departure had reached its peak, she returned. Without warning, she appeared at the door and slipped inside the coach. She pushed the items from her seat and collapsed upon the bench. Steam rose from her body as she exhaled great clouds to match, completely winded and nearly exhausted.

"Here," she managed to croak, handing a sealed envelope to Voltaire. "Just... a moment..." She swallowed heavily before bounding back through the door of the coach, closing it behind her this time. The sounds of retching were heard just outside.

The door opened slowly. She breathed easier as she returned, but sweat stood out on her exposed brow and upper lip. "I apologize..."

Voltaire still hadn't said a word. He appeared to mentally assemble an inquiry, but failed. The drivers, too astonished to speak, were also silent.

Looking in turn at each one of her companions, Seramis gestured for the men to give her room. "Gentlemen, I require every inch of space within this coach that you can spare." Her tone was commanding, and all—even Voltaire—quickly shrank against the far side of the coach.

In a blur of speed only hinted at by any known definition of the concept, Seramis transformed her appearance back into that of a fashionable noble courtesan. The gowns seemed to float in the middle of the air as Seramis slid herself into them, instead of pulling them over herself. The face paint disappeared and powder and rouge were applied in an instant, too fast for any of the men to clearly follow. The wig flew from its hidden compartment and was put neatly into place upon her head.

Seramis settled and looked at the results in a mirror, deftly applying touches of powder to hide the perspiration which had been so prevalent just moments earlier. In that instant, squads of city guards ran up to the conveyances lining the entrance to the city. At each carriage and coach, a knocking at the door preceded demands for inspection.

But Voltaire and Seramis merely appeared to be vain and bored travelers, a merchant and a courtesan, who calmly and nonchalantly presented their papers, sending the city guards rushing onward into the night in search of a lone figure fleeing from pursuit.

At the guard's departure, Seramis collapsed deeper into the seat. "Despite all appearances, I can report success. Please take the pass that I gave you earlier to the captain of the gate.

He will take it, and within the hour, we shall be escorted within the city gates. But I pray you, please let me rest first." Sweat reappeared upon her brow, as it had only been briefly hidden by the powder, and she sank further into a slouch.

"But, what was all that? How did you manage?" Voltaire asked, the words rushing forth, his thoughts practically inchoate. He also appeared to exhibit a newly formed respect for Seramis, or maybe even for women in general.

"You did say that, once we reached Paris, men would be chasing me." Lady Seramis managed to whisper before closing her eyes and drawing her gowns over herself, instantly asleep.

Father Time had not been idle, as Hanaawa was far from the only dream catcher trying to trap him. They were desperate to stop the nightly onslaught of nightmares and horrifying visitations the wraith cast about. But to some of his victims, Father Time's visits were almost welcome, despite being dark, violent, and painful. For the slaves and the oppressed natives, the dispossessed wanderers and the poor punished by transport to the colonies for the crime of stealing to eat, Father Time presented his nightly visits as opportunities.

Night after night, while some were tormented by terrifying scenes of violence and anguish, others were gifted with beatific and pastoral scenes of freedom and liberation and justice restored. Over time, however, even these dreams became a sort of torture. The bright nightly visions that appeared for some contrasted cruelly with the shadowy reality that dawned with each pale sunrise.

Instead of providing a nightly escape from the harshness of their existence, the dreams turned upon the dreamers with accusations that such bliss would never be theirs by their own doing. In the shadows of their dreams, Father Time whispered they deserved their lot and were unworthy of redemption. Justice and luxury were denied them because they were weak, feckless, and passive. He twisted their feelings until they had no choice but to take up arms and revolt.

He exhorted the weak and downtrodden to rise up, whereafter all the pleasures and true justice denied for so long would be theirs for the taking. In their dreams, Father Time became the overseer cracking the whip, the settler stealing land, the foreman banishing idle workers, and the magistrate casting judgment. Each night, he thus imposed himself between the low and their expected reward.

By day, Father Time quoted the Bard.

"*What would you have, you curs;*
That like nor peace nor war?
The one affrights you,
The other makes you proud."

He talked to himself as he walked along the middle of a trail towards a plantation, while a mule-drawn cart slowly passed over his head. He had shrunk himself to just a fraction over six inches tall, so he easily moved under the axles. At this scale, the cart appeared to be almost stuck or frozen in time, pulled by an animal easily mistaken for one standing still. With little effort, he rushed past the raised hoof of the animal as it descended slowly to the ground.

Reduced as he was to this scale, time moved slowly as the being once known as Patrick Tempus rushed through the days. He walked from opportunity to opportunity, still unseen but—in comparison to his victims—unbelievably fast. To pass the time while he walked, he concocted schemes of how he would make his old enemies suffer. Between such musings he indulged in recalling the more vituperative lines of his favorite poems and plays.

Day after day, Father Time undermined colonial institutions and social structures by one invisible deed after another. Over and over, he would steal and misplace arms and munitions from dozens upon dozens of plantations and farms, but not so many from any one place as to be noticed. He then strategically distributed them. In some cases, he carefully placed the weapons where they would be stumbled upon by those he incited to rebellion. Invisible to both his victims and his dupes, Father Time did the work of a hundred spies from the Carolinas to Virginia Colony, striding amongst his victims unnoticed but not unfelt.

And each night, even as he inspired the oppressed to rise up, he exhorted the owners and overseers to brutally and violently smash them down. Each night, he would taunt the slave owners,

"You souls of geese,
That bear the shapes of men, how have you run;
From slaves that apes would beat!"

The next day, scores of slaves and servants throughout the colonies were punished and some even killed for petty or purely imagined offenses at the hands of their enraged masters. Father Time smiled at this, knowing that his work would be magnified by each incident, and stoke the fires of rebellion that he tended.

When the spark struck and took hold in the tinder of raw emotion on every side, Father Time reveled in the business that followed. Appearing as a scout or runaway slave, he would appear to a group of natives or slaves and counsel them to pick up the arms he had cached and then go hide themselves. He promised them in turn a group of militia or overseers would be headed directly towards them.

More often than not, the militia was not heading for the obvious trap. With a mere thought, Father Time would be able to transform his appearance to whatever he wished. So he would appear to them disguised as an officer returning from a skirmish, desperately seeking reinforcements. He would plead, beg, or cajole them to join in battle—of course, in the direction he wished them to go.

He found that he could appear to certain individuals alone, and all others around his intended could neither see nor hear the exchange. After leading the militia in the general direction he wished, he could claim to walk ahead and lie to them about the absence of traps or hidden warriors. To the watching natives, it was as if the militia listened to ghosts, pausing to listen to unheard instructions.

And Father Time was that ghost unheard by the natives, telling the militia to wait in the clearing that was to be their final resting place. Then, unheard by the soldiers, he would shout to the natives and the carnage would begin. In the aftermath, he would trip up deserters, or reveal the cowards in hiding—there was always at least one—calling out to the natives to come claim their victims. But he made sure that at least one of them would be left alive to spread the tale of horror and stoke the fires of reprisal.

Rarely did he have to personally intervene after the initial organized resistance was routed. He simply wanted to ensure that the revolt continued where so many others had previously died out. He evened the playing field by day, so to speak, after he had added fuel to the fire through the night.

In all, it was the most perfect thing that Father Time had ever experienced. The moans and groans of the wounded and the dying were like sonorous calls to slumber for him, although he had no need of sleep. The clash of arms, the crash of fighting, and the roaring of guns were like intoxicating wine to him, although he had no desire to drink. And the flames from the burning farms and towns, the funeral pyres on the edge of civilization, equally lighting the shadowy days and nights, removed the quotidian division of time so that all things appeared insignificant at all times. These flames were a feast for him: a feast upon which he gorged greedily.

Colonel McClure stood watch atop the roof at Helleborine Hall, bundled against the cold. Musket in hand, he watched with a steely gaze as the glow on the southern horizon grew. His grip tightened as he scanned for evidence of the roving bands of native warriors that had already begun to raid Henrico County. For now the only disaster to strike one of the neighboring properties was the slave revolt at the plantation to the south of the James River. Brooke's Farm to the east was also spared from the worst, being a simple family estate like the freehold that he now defended.

While the mill on the Helleborine property was busy, it apparently hadn't attracted the attention of the native warriors that raided the mines farther inland to the west above the Fall Line. Not for the mineral wealth but for the tools did the natives attack the mines, removing whatever they could carry.

The fiery glow worried him. Despite the lieutenant governor's extensive military experience and well-trained militia, his troops had apparently fallen to the raiders. The colonel was reasonably sure that an uncoordinated assault upon an organized defense wouldn't succeed. He weighed the options: either the assault was more coordinated than he had been led to believe, or the defenses were more disorganized than Lieutenant Governor Gooch should have allowed.

Either prospect worried the colonel as he looked over his own defenses, with his men positioned behind earthwork barricades that encircled the buildings. He hadn't time to build a protective wall as he had half-suggested to Lady Seramis—*But why stop there? Why not dig an entire moat? Why not build bastions and fill them with artillery?* Colonel McClure stopped his internal questioning with that last question, as he would have actually felt reasonably secure in a fortress. And at present, he truly wished he had built one, however unfeasible it would have been to actually complete said castle before the disaster that was now unfolding.

Just as he was starting another line of wishful thinking while he scanned the tree line surrounding the household, one of the older men slowly climbed up the ladder leading to the roof.

"Lemuel?" McClure asked, "What are you doing?"

"Sir, reporting for watch. You're relieved." The older man could still bellow, despite his age.

"I am no such thing," the colonel said almost as loud.

"Well, roast my chestnuts and skin my hare, but only by your wife's word would I say you're wrong." Lemuel continued to shout as the colonel smiled in response.

"I'll have no truck with that—" McClure fell silent, staring at the line of trees to the west. Holding his hand up for quiet, he whistled like a jaybird, the alarm for a sign of motion to the west. It was only a flutter in the trees that had caught his attention, lasting less than a second, but it was enough.

Staring at the trees, McClure thought that no animal would normally have caused the undergrowth to rustle like that without some accompanying noise, but a person trying to move stealthily and failing momentarily would have made just that kind of mistake before recovering. From his vantage point, he could see the fourths of the four-man squads he had trained quietly moving from their reserves to reinforce the western-facing barricades.

Whispering to Lemuel, McClure asked him to continue to watch the west while he looked around. What if the motion was a mere feint meant to distract us before an attack from another direction?

"Sir, you need to see this," whispered Lemuel. The colonel whirled around at the concern in Lemuel's voice and was amazed at what he saw.

Looking back to Lemuel, he said, "On three?" With an affirming nod, he started, "One. Two..."

"EVERYBODY HOLD!" The two bellowed together, and were likely heard for miles around.

"I now hope you will be staying up here for a bit, Lemuel, while I see what's going on," Colonel McClure said and scrambled down the ladders to the ground below, leaving Lemuel to gaze incomprehensibly at the dozens if not hundreds of little children stepping into the fields from the forests beyond, led by a single, tall black woman, with two infants in her arms, and many more in the arms of the older children besides.

The woman's name was Nalia, and Mrs. McClure spoke with her at length while the maids guided the children out of the cold and into the barn, where it was a little warmer. That his wife had already started assessing and managing the situation was no surprise to Colonel McClure, who arrived to hear her offer temporary lodging for the visitors.

"Cy," she said as her husband approached, "you'll want to hear this." She smoothed her apron before warming her hands in the pockets of her cotton dress.

"Now, Sarah, my goodwife, if you wish me to, I will."

"I trust you both," Hanaawa said as he approached, "and I want to hear it just the same, if you don't mind." When no objection was made, he continued, "What is the news? Where did these children come from?"

"Some from as far away as Shenandoah, and there are more on their way," Mrs. McClure began. "They've been abandoned as the slaves who fight rise up against their overseers, leaving women and children defenseless against the marauding bands that seem to be everywhere."

"Father Time is doing his work," Hanaawa announced, looking pained at the news.

"Are you speaking figuratively, or are you referring to that man who captured Lady Seramis?" McClure asked.

"Once, he was that, Colonel," Hanaawa answered. "But he is no mere man anymore."

The look of disbelief on McClure's face was evident. "I know you've described wonders and terrors that I can't imagine, but tell me: if he's no man, then what is he?"

"I wish I knew! I can only tell you that I saw him disappear before my eyes on the deck of the airship. Furthermore, I just felt his presence in a dream. You can call him what you like, but I call him enemy."

"But, Hanaawa," Mrs. McClure said gently, "How do you prepare for that kind of enemy? How do you fight something that can get into your very dreams—and an enemy who could do that would explain a lot of what I have dreamt lately—and disappear?"

"He is not here now—" Hanaawa started.

"How can you be sure?" McClure asked.

"I have felt his presence before, Colonel," Hanaawa raised a hand as he finished, deflecting further debate. "I think we're getting a little off-track, and I apologize for bringing up the subject."

"That's very gracious, but you can bring up anything you like," Mrs. McClure said. "If you think it's important, we'll listen to you, no longer how long it takes!"

"Let's talk about it some more, soon," McClure said before turning to his wife. "Why did you want me to hear the news, Missus?"

"Because we can't stay here, Mister," Mrs. McClure answered with a grin that quickly vanished. "We're about to be overrun—not by aggressors but by refugees. Nalia took the abandoned children from her plantation at the first sign of trouble, and more joined her the farther she walked towards Williamsburg. But more women along with the old and infirm, and of course far more children, are just behind her. Of every hue and every station, the victims of this rebellion are fleeing their indefensible homes and heading to the coast seeking protection or escape."

Colonel McClure's eyes went wide. "And if they're driven from the roads by marauders, then they will stop at the river and follow it to the coast—right through our gates!"

"If we try to send them all on their way"—Mrs. McClure put a gentle hand on her husband—"and wash our hands of it, we will be as guilty as if we committed the crimes ourselves, should they be attacked."

The Fury of Storms

"And we can't let them stay here," Colonel McClure said. "We'll be overrun as you said, running out of food and essentials when the numbers grow too many."

"What if we could send them to Williamsburg with an escort?" Hanaawa proposed.

"That would leave us too few defenders..." Colonel McClure was thoughtful.

"For a siege, yes. But not"—she looked up into her husband's eyes—"for an evacuation."

PART TWO: The World, Dying

Could White Apple be the Great Mother Sun?

Chapter Six: A Contrast

In which differences are stark

The Comte du Chevalier, hosting Dame Seramis and Voltaire—traveling under their respective *noms d'espionnage*, Catherine Dunoyer and Sir Thomas Cheltenham—assured them that the library would gladly copy any item in its collection, for a small fee. They had to pass on the opportunity, sadly.

Of course, Voltaire was wearing a disguise, as he was well known in Paris. He had never visited the Palais Bibliothèque des découvertes géographiques when he had lived there, although he was familiar enough with the famous landmark. On the outside the library was built like a stone fortress, as if intended to preserve the contents from attack. But inside, the numerous candelabra revealed polished marble floors and brass everywhere. Surrounded by sumptuous luxury, they had agreed to meet their contact in the French Foreign Service here, hoping to avoid any of Voltaire's old enemies—or worse, his friends.

While they browsed the collection, their host left to complete some correspondence, leaving Seramis and Voltaire alone. Seramis was once again dressed in the highest of fashion, her gown resplendent in satin ribbons and lace, leaving her shoulders bare, although she wore a cape when they were about in the city. The curls of her wig were powdered, as was her face, in a soft white.

"Well, Mademoiselle Dunoyer?" Voltaire spoke English carefully, in a broad Yorkshire accent, as the caps upon his teeth tended to slip if stressed.

"*Oui, monsieur*?" Seramis replied, stifling laughter at the bushy eyebrows and false whiskers Voltaire wore—they looked quite real, even to her practiced eye.

"Are you rested after your travels?"

"*Oui, je me suis reposeé*," she agreed, hoping her French passed casual inspection.

Leaning in closer he whispered, "What did you do last night?"

"*Êtes-vous jaloux*?" she asked, teasing him as if he were a jealous lover. She then tapped his shoulder with her fan and then pointed to the only other patron, an elderly gentleman scanning map after map. Whispering, she drew nearly head to head with him. "You are just upset that you haven't heard the latest gossip? About the attempt on the life of the dauphin?"

"What? The prince? When?"

"*Oui*," she said, momentarily forgetting that she could speak English openly. "It was days ago causing the city to be closed completely. The prince had gambling debts..." She leaned back, smiling.

"Ah!" Voltaire said, "Well, it's hardly polite for me to continue questioning you on this matter, so I'll leave it be...." There had been no time for them to talk last night when admitted into the city in the presence of the guards that accompanied them. And their apartments in their host's household were in separate wings, naturally, so it had only been just now that Voltaire's curiosity overcame his discretion and led him to ask about the previous night.

With his curiosity partially satisfied—and with the elderly visitor having left the two alone in the library—he and Seramis took to the tomes, books, scrolls, and maps with passion. They sought answers to the questions of air currents (When will the dark clouds dissipate?), population displacement (Where will millions of people go if Northern Europe becomes uninhabitable?), and other questions in rapid-fire discussion until their contact—who used the codename Deucalion—arrived.

The price of their admittance into this underground society was paid immediately in the currency of espionage—information, when Seramis described to him the origin and composition of the dark clouds—leaving out her own personal part in the story as well as any mention of Father Time. The older gentleman listened attentively, asking questions about what they learned in the Library and if they could speculate on the specific origin of the particulates.

"Origin?" Seramis asked. "Why, the particulates originated from the island of Bermuda itself—the very land was distorted by the pull and the transformation of the earth into the great pillar."

"Of course!" Deucalion agreed. His pale skin matched his powdered wig. "And this towering column of earth? I understand that you said you could neither comprehend nor relate to how it came to be, but you said it was tall enough that it could be seen from over the horizon? From a ship, I presume? What was the name of the ship you mentioned?"

"I heard no name of any ship, good sir," Voltaire interjected, smiling. "Your genius in the area of questioning is evident, but the price we negotiated for this interview and subsequent contact was limited only to information about the dark clouds that threaten us all—uniting us in common purpose."

"Forgive me! Old habits, of course..." He rose and called for his servants to fetch their greatcoats and Seramis's cape in preparation to leave. "But please remember that the same calamity that unites some in common purpose is also seen as a source of fresh opportunities for individual promotion by others."

Dame Seramis answered coolly, "Those who seek their own individual promotion in the face of annihilation would hasten the destruction of us all."

"But like rats on a sinking ship," Deucalion added, "they will turn on each other in desperation, ignorant of the effect their actions have upon the group."

"As you said," Voltaire added. "Old habits."

Deucalion led them to a laboratory where they were able to work in the manner in which Dame Seramis truly excelled. She had been delighted at the collection in the library, where she had easily devoured most of its content in a few hours. After a light lunch to refresh herself, she plunged into work at the lab and could have spent several days therein before exhausting the possibilities of the material and herself in the process.

Exchanging her gowns and wig for a coat of canvas, miller's cap, and gloves, she went straight to work. She joined the assistants at the tables while the gentlemen stood at the benches that lined the walls. She quickly found that she had preceded her French cousins into the air by only a few years at best—decades at worst—given the standard political climate and waste of resources the ceaseless continental wars would consume.

The French had apparently seen or heard of the same plans she had found in Lisbon, and it seemed that several groups were attempting to work out the problem of buoyancy. It occurred to Seramis while working that there were a number of promising routes to explore on the production of the hydrogolic compound, but as exploring that particular gas had led to the destruction of her home, she thought it best not to share that avenue of research.

But upon recalling her recent work on the pile that safely stored the electrical discharge of lightning as they walked over to a large capacitor and electrostatic generator, Seramis was struck by inspiration. The working of the sphere of the electrostatic generator and its corona effect became the subject of intense discussion as the group slowly argued the dialectic of storing and generating electrical current.

Voltaire and Deucalion joined in the discussion, and the workers drew up plans that replaced the ceramic of Seramis's capacitor with glass, lined with metal and filled with a copper solution and using the curled metal rod, but rotated in the direction of the flow of the current. This led to the misunderstanding amongst several of the group that electricity was a fluid. Seramis had not the desire to correct them upon the literal use of what was—to her—a conceptual breakthrough in the understanding of all forms of the transfer of energy. However, with the breakthrough, it was clearly time to celebrate.

That evening, a simple salon had been transformed into a masquerade, echoing the changes amongst the aristocracy in France, and indeed, throughout Europe. What were once simple social functions instead became elaborate events; elaborate events grew in complexity to become festivities; and festivities combined every manner in elaborate entertainment to become breathless spectacles. A small circle of friends, formerly having scheduled a meeting to discuss arts and sciences, had added to their social calendar a masquerade in its place.

Wearing an elaborate mask to the event, Voltaire could now converse with his countrymen in his native tongue, although to Lady Seramis hearing him speak French was not as distracting as the intensely clashing checquered waistcoat and striped breeches that he wore. For her part, even Lady Seramis's wig was tied in ribbons, while fake flowers were sewn into her gown by her host's maids. Instead of the full-faced mask that Voltaire wore, Lady Seramis carried a hand-held one with costume jewelry upon one side and soft velvet on the other to rest against her face.

Voltaire repeated the tale of the source of the scourge that darkened the skies, while Lady Seramis listened in drowsy acknowledgment. While gentlemen kept introducing themselves to her, having chaperones in the form of garrulous Voltaire and the taciturn Deucalion was sufficient to distract their interest. The evening wore upon her, but Seramis didn't feel the same anguish or restless stirrings that had nearly driven her to distraction when she previously attended social events. Instead, she relaxed and found an inner calm while listening to the long, drawn out descriptions of the fateful events that lead to the darkened skies that devastated Europe. Also, unbidden, but not without a clear cause, the image of Henry helped Seramis bear the more wilting moments of the conversation, his kind and strong features a welcome anchor to the headlong rush with which she pursued this venture.

After the visits with the nobility, Seramis retired to her apartments and had just prepared herself for sleep when a knock on the door and a whispered entreaty announced Voltaire. Shaking her head at the lost sleep, she went to let him inside, but had to suppress a giggle when he entered the room, closing the door behind him.

Seramis could scarcely withhold her glee. "I thought the effect of your garments earlier to be simple moddishness, but I see from this garb that you have started a completely new style!" The last words dissolved into hearty laughter as she doubled over, hands over her stomach.

"What? I simply modeled my own garb after yours from yesterday evening as we have a further mission to achieve tonight!"

"Mission?"

The sight of Voltaire wearing black hose, short black breeches, coat and kerchief tied over his head in the style of a Barbary pirate was simply impossible to take seriously. Yet the idea of running about Paris for a second consecutive night was more than enough to shock Seramis into sobriety.

"Get in your garb as you call it," Voltaire decreed. "We're about to save a priceless contribution to culture and obtain copies of the collected manuscripts of the keyboard works of Jean-Baptiste Lully, whose health is deteriorating." Voltaire had definitely attracted Seramis's interest. "But first, might I make a request?"

"What is it?" she asked.

"I had no idea its usefulness until you demonstrated it." He shuffled his feet, gaze downcast, then looked directly at her and blurted out his request. "Could I use—you know, for painting my face the same as yours—your *maquillage*?"

Mrs. McClure examined the refugees as they arrived before organizing traveling parties and sending them on their way again. Their condition, allowing for travel, grew worse as time went on. Of course, many hadn't survived to make it this far. But the memories of the fallen were kept alive in the tales told by the survivors. In their innocence and naiveté they tried to understand the horrors as well as they could, by talking with Mrs. McClure about their experiences as she tended them.

The news she heard from the most recent arrivals seemed impossible, but in these times was more likely to be real than not. Calling for her husband, she explained, "Cyrus, as much as I dreamed of the coming day of abolition, I never wanted slavery to be burned out at the root with such violence!"

Colonel McClure had arrived at the barn on the Helleborine estate, armed and dressed for travel at a moment's notice. "What do you mean, Sarah?" He was concerned for his wife, as she appeared distraught and nearly frantic, when she had been so cool and organized the last time he had seen her.

"I just heard from the last of the refugees—"

"Pardon my interruption, but how can you know that they are the last?" Colonel McClure asked.

"They told me again and again that the remnants of the militia, the soldiers that they thought would protect them, have joined with the surviving overseers to hunt down and kill every slave and every native they find." Mrs. McClure sobbed with the news. "They're killing men, women and children in a race war, Cy."

"Dear Sarah, I've never seen you like this." Colonel McClure comforted his wife. "You've been through so much,

I've always thought that you were like the rock that the breaking waves could neither move nor impress with all their fury."

"And I've never seen anything like this, Cy." She broke down entirely, shoulders shaking, voice shattered. "There won't be any more refugees because whole plantations and whole villages are being slaughtered to the last slave or last native!" She gestured at the piles of bloody bandages, the stacks of cut-away rags that were sometimes all that the refugees wore upon their arrival. "What good is all this effort? We've got to stop this somehow!"

Hanaawa entered the barn, pushing a wheelbarrow. Without hesitation, he grabbed a pitchfork and set about dumping the old clothes and bandages into it for burning.

"Leave it!" shouted Mrs. McClure. "Just leave it," she spoke more quietly as she walked to him. "I'm done. We're through." She grabbed the pitchfork from his hands and tossed it away. "This is over! It's finished."

Hanaawa was silent. Colonel McClure put down his gun and moved, arms outstretched, to hold his wife.

"No. Good husband, this is not time for gentleness." She held up her hands. "Everything and everyone—our whole culture—is dying, and I no longer want to heal its wounds and prolong the suffering. I only want to hasten the inevitable end, if it has finally come to this."

"We have been pushed to this end." Hanaawa spoke softly and reasonably, trying to console her. "Prejudice and bigotry may be at the core of who some—maybe even most—people are. But nearly everyone just wants to love their family, know they belong, and keep the peace." As Mrs. McClure listened to him her composure returned. "This is indeed your worst nightmare come true, as you value so highly the natural order of a balanced life. But the balance has been turned over by Father Time, and there is no order to any of this—only chaos."

While Hanaawa spoke, Sarah collapsed into her husband's embrace.

He continued even as her eyes closed gently. "You've felt the disturbance in your dreams, and you know that this is no natural turn of events. The darkness that has shrouded our world from horizon to horizon is mirrored by a darkness that weighs upon our spirits."

Hanaawa's speech became a spell of healing and he held up his hands to channel his energies, which formed a rhythm in his words, flowing in and around the three of them as they stood alone in the barn.

"But you can resist falling into shadow yourself." He spoke more gently still, and the sing-song words found purchase upon the thin stretches of Mrs. McClure's troubled soul.

"Your inner light, burning so brightly,
Healing and guiding so many, can never be stamped out,
If you shelter it true, from winds of hate that tear at you.
But if you feel that your light fades, tormented by shades,
Dimming from doubt and fear; we'll be here, always near,
Inspired by hope that is true."

The susurrant echo of the words faded, but a new light shone in Hanaawa's eyes, as words from a source beyond himself flowed into him.

"*She who heals those wounded by hate, inspires all others, while guided by fate!*"

Colonel McClure gently took his wife up into his arms, as she had fallen asleep standing just where she was. Wide-eyed at Hanaawa's power, he whispered, "You must teach me how to do that some time."

Relieved by what had just transpired, Hanaawa whispered in kind, concern darkening his already near-black eyes. "I can't claim any special knowledge. I think it's this barn, as this isn't the first time—"

"I know—I was there!" McClure agreed. "But it's time for us to go now, isn't it?"

"I just hope there's still time." Hanaawa held open the barn door for the colonel as he carried his wife from the building.

"Time for what?" Colonel McClure asked.

"I have no idea but I think we're going to find out," Hanaawa said as he lowered the crossbar.

By the time the last of Lady Seramis's household had arrived, Jamestown and Williamsburg were in flames. Raids and pitched battles had left their mark in nearly every quarter. The travelers from New Helleborine Hall, including Hanaawa and Colonel and Mrs. McClure, arrived unmolested, as they were too well armed for the smaller bands of marauding natives who attacked by stealth, and too poor for the organized militias who confiscated bullion and tobacco or any other wealth. For all outward appearances, they were only carrying a musical instrument as well as some traveling rations in addition to the clothes on their backs. The few remnants of local governance were scattering, and individual militia leaders had set up their own fiefdoms and became warlords in all but in name.

Just as the travelers were about to devise some means of communicating with the *Agility*, Captain de Ibarra and White Apple, escorted by some of the crew, found them.

"While I thank providence and your skill for your safety, I know the timing is no coincidence." The captain spoke loud enough to be heard above the cries of the bereaved and the shouts of the enraged in the constant din and chaos that was the remains of Williamsburg.

"Uncle!" White Apple shouted, as she and Hanaawa were reunited. Tears of joy streamed down his face, betraying his typical stoic demeanor. For her part, she smiled but stiffened in his embrace.

"Obviously, we could no longer stay—" Colonel McClure started.

"Obviously, neither could we," the captain said.

"Where to, gentlemen?" Mrs. McClure affected calm, but her glances betrayed her nervousness.

"I see ye've got the rest of the household," Ibarra observed. "The others you sent as escorts with the refugees have already been brought aboard, along with a few more refugees who have no place to go."

"Wait 'til you see what I've made!" White Apple said, grinning brightly.

Adjusting his tricorn, the captain smiled. "You speak of the mutilation of my ship as if you're proud of it. But let's see what happens now." He turned to the McClures. "We've been a bit busy, or I would've sent for ye sooner." Winking, he gestured to the gig, beached and ready for loading. "Let's get aboard," he shouted, as the crew began unpacking the animals and the wagon. Everything seemed in order until he spied an unusual crate. "What in the seven seas is that?"

"Just one of Lady Seramis's personal belongings. I think it's a musical instrument." Mrs. McClure was coy. She knew that the instrument was her mistress's hidden treasure, and was determined to protect it. And protecting it meant maintaining the secret.

"Of all her things, and in the midst of an entire world descending in chaos, why'd ye think to bring that?" The captain froze in his perplexity, when all around him was descending into chaos.

"It seemed like a good idea," Colonel McClure answered, equally discreetly. "It may not mean a thing, or it might mean a great deal. I'm sure it has some sentimental value...."

"Well, as long as we have our priorities in order." Captain de Ibarra's sarcasm chilled the space between them as he resumed shepherding the others onto the ship. "Shall we leave this place?"

Mrs. McClure hesitated.

"I don't mean to put too fine a point on it, but from what I've heard, ye've been luckier than any one has a right to be getting through that unscathed." He nodded to the orange glow on the horizon in the perpetual twilight.

"I agree, Captain," Mrs. McClure said. She looked at Hanaawa. "We really have been altogether too lucky—if you can call it luck. It's just a feeling I have...."

"I have the same feeling—like we've been guided here, or we've been left to our own devices on purpose," Hanaawa said. "Not for our own goals, but for someone or something else."

"Well then," the captain said, rolling his eyes, "we could just stand here and wait for that purpose to show up and kick us in the shins and tell us to get moving—or, we could get the household and refugees to the estate that once belonged to that old dog, De La Warr. You might have heard of it. Around here, it's called Delaware."

Chapter Seven: A Passion

In which a first kiss precedes a trap

After rescuing the musical manuscripts from the greedy lawyers preying upon the sickly Jean-Baptiste Lully, Voltaire and Lady Seramis were surprised to discover that the identity of Deucalion was actually that of the court organist, Jean-Philippe Rameau. Rameau had shed his cover immediately upon being asked to preserve the music of France's most revered composer. He hadn't known of any danger to the scores and personally copied them when Voltaire asked if he knew of anyone who could discreetly undertake a mission of musical preservation. Rameau then became crucial in persuading ministers of state and their patrons to seek peace with England and form a new alliance to preserve their culture in the face of the disaster that had befallen them all.

With success apparently as their new starting point, leaving Paris was not nearly as difficult as entering had been. Voltaire and Seramis no longer had to maintain the pretense of their assumed identities while they traveled east towards Rheims, Strasbourg, and eventually Stuttgart for the next leg of their journey. Their goal was even farther east, as they set their sights upon Berlin. The little company had grown; King George II had sent four additional men-at-arms (secretly carrying letters for the safe conduct of Voltaire and Seramis through Prussia) and an additional coach from London. They provisioned themselves for the weeks of travel ahead as the never-ending winter grew ever more intense. Of course, there was no guarantee that they would find food or shelter even upon a once-heavily trafficked highway.

Voltaire had offered to travel separately in the newly arrived coach, allowing Seramis some privacy, but she had grown accustomed to his presence. Time spent in each other's company passed quickly, despite the monotony of the snowfall. Speaking softly but swiftly, Seramis and Voltaire would complete each other's sentences as they spoke. Soon, they even turned to composing pairs of sonnets in turn, sharing the results back and forth after they composed each line.

Often, she would feign ignorance, but would otherwise be keenly aware of his bold expression and attentive gaze. For her part, her thoughts dwelled less and less upon the expressions of attraction from Albion as time went by. Even the picture of him in her mind's eye started to blur the features of both Voltaire and him into a single, somewhat confusing image.

Other thoughts also played about Seramis's memories, adding to her doubts, as she remembered the infatuation she had quite keenly felt—although never acknowledged—for Innes, the minion to that master manipulator, Father Time. Unfortunately, thoughts of Innes and her memories of traveling as one half of a seemingly inseparable pair intruded when Voltaire would simply smile at her while listening. It was evident from how his expression changed that Seramis's concern must have been apparent, as he would quickly cast his eyes downward and reassemble his expression into a more neutral aspect.

Voltaire's feelings were far from neutral, however. As the companions huddled within their individual traveling capes after one breakfast, he accidentally blurted out in response to a question regarding the Socratic dialectic, "Such a woman as you I never imagined existed in reality, despite dreaming of you all of my life!"

Seramis started to speak, but words actually failed her, torn as she was between basking in the glow of Voltaire's praise and shying away from the heat of his passion. It was a perfect moment, to her perception a broad expanse within which she actually welcomed time's standing still. Seramis stared openly at Voltaire's fine features, while slipping into the rhythm of his gentle words. Warmth flooded her being despite the freezing temperatures, until the feelings grew in intensity to the point of being almost unwelcome.

"Monsieur!" Seramis gasped and looked away, her breathing rapid and shallow as her head swam with the giddiness of a simple blush.

"My dear!" Voltaire exclaimed, throwing off his cape and reaching for her. "What's the matter?"

She raised her hands to stop him, but in the close confines of the coach, she had pushed away her own blankets and found herself gently touching his solid chest rather than pushing him away. She turned back and saw such concern and openness in his eyes that she could see nothing else but his face before her. His arms naturally came to rest upon hers. Where they touched, she felt an electric thrum, pulsing softly but insistently. As the current seemingly passed between them, Voltaire and Seramis obeyed the natural law of attraction as surely as opposing magnetic poles. Breathing in unison, they slowly but inevitably leaned into each other.

Fluttering momentarily, Lady Seramis's eyes closed as she strained her neck forward slightly. The sweet shock of the kiss jolted her in a conflicting but perfectly desirable mix of Voltaire's rough stubble and his tender lips upon her own soft mouth and downy cheek. The rush of humours and blood magnified the sensations a thousandfold at every single solitary spot upon her lips. The jolt sent a tiny and nearly unnoticeable shiver into the very core of her, where it grew and shuddered, flooding her body with a radiant glow. As Voltaire gently pressed his lips against hers, Seramis pressed back insistently. She welcomed the feel of his hands upon her face and the back of her head, almost as if their gentle touch kept her head above water even as she felt as if she were drowning.

Their first kiss lasted just a moment, frozen in time. In that infinite scale of human kindness, Seramis and Voltaire could have deeply bonded—indeed, on one level they did. They might have found a true and abiding love in the rush of emotions that had only been amplified by their communion, had they not had a more pressing and dire need. After a moment, the sweet spell of the kiss was mutually and simultaneously suspended in them both. Even as they had connected on some profound level, they both knew that they had just crossed a line where discretion alone could preserve their partnership.

If they wished to continue upon their mission, they would have to step back from that line, but not immediately and only far enough to maintain their objectivity. Satiating their desire for human companionship in one sense, but fearful of fueling their passion for a more perfect union, they slowly broke apart. With smiles upon their faces they looked at each other breathlessly, having shared a tender and sensitive rapport, a new-found intimacy as Voltaire now knew the sweet taste of Seramis's tender lips. And she, in turn, had opened the veil of passion to a completely new experience.

Unlike Paris, Berlin wasn't closed for entry, but entrance to the city appeared to be disrupted just the same. Voltaire and Seramis had no idea of the cause of the problems, but—once again—they found themselves slowing down the closer they came to their goal. The chaos was unlike any social upheaval she had ever seen; Seramis stared in wonder at the crowds that filled the main highway as they moved slowly from Spandau in the west. Coaches and carts full of burghers, waldgrafs, and minor nobility were leaving Berlin in droves, while pouring into the city were the numberless poor, stepping off the road temporarily to let the coaches bearing Voltaire and Seramis and their guards pass them by. None of the traffic moved efficiently in the sepulchral twilight that was the best the daylight would offer, and the snowfall muted the sounds of the multitude, lending a dreamlike quality to the current leg of their journey.

"Today is the first day of summer, 1731," Voltaire said to Seramis as they rode into Berlin, "and all this upheaval can't be a coincidence."

"We didn't hear of any proclamation during our stay in Brandenburg," she replied. "It would have been helpful if we could have met with the margravia, who, as I mentioned, is King George II's sister. She would have been able to fill in the gaps in our knowledge of local politics." Lady Seramis had truly missed seeing her friend and benefactor, the Princess Sophie Dorothea.

"We may have simply missed any announcements," Voltaire said. "But what is the purpose of displacing so many people?" Unfolding a letter, he continued. "We are supposed to present our credentials at the palace, but if we can find no nobles within Berlin to support our cause..." His voice trailed away as he looked again to the highway, and saw his opportunities driven away with the exodus.

"If we fail here, we have to choose," she said. "Do we go back to Brandenburg, and try to find allies loyal to the royal family? Do we go back farther east to Düsseldorf? Or, do we pursue these fleeing nobles to whatever sanctuary they seek?"

"Or," he said, "do we give up on Prussia altogether? We could try for the elector of Saxony, if he's in Dresden—"

"But if he's in Warsaw," she interrupted, wistful in her contemplation, "it would take weeks to get there!"

"You're right, we should try to find out where he is before trudging across Europe! Especially since you and I have nothing in common and absolutely no way to pass the time —"

"I hear the other coach is very nice," Seramis said conversationally.

"You wish to travel in it?" He raised one eyebrow and smiled.

Still serious, she said, "Oh, no, I wouldn't want to displace the other drivers. But you should try it; pass the time with like-gendered company and all that."

"Do you really mean it?" he blurted, eyes wide in alarm.

Rolling her eyes, Seramis said, "I suppose not." Smiling, she turned to him. "I've gotten used to having you around."

After they had arrived at the Berliner Schloss, Voltaire and Seramis presented their credentials to the majordomo and waited, fully expecting simultaneously to be summarily dismissed and courteously invited to apply for an audience that would never happen until they could influence someone favorable to King Frederick Wilhelm. Voltaire attempted to make some conversation, but either his accent or his amiability proved insufficient to make a dent in the stony silence that surrounded them.

While admiring the portraits hung in close concentration about the Main Hall, Voltaire and Seramis had inadvertently wandered away from the center of the room where they were expected to wait. They were surprised by the far inner doors opening slightly, yielding a single figure without servants or attendants: a woman in a resplendently embroidered gown, carrying her own flowing train in one hand as she pushed open the door, looking around the room expectedly.

"Princess Sophie Dorothea!" Lady Seramis cried at the sight of the newly arrived Margravia of Brandenburg, sister of King George II, and wife to Prussia's King Frederick Wilhelm. She was dressed much more conservatively than when Seramis had seen her last—in Lisbon, so long ago. The princess wore a lace veil and dark shawls covering her shoulders. Picking up the hem of her gown, Seramis ran across the room, but froze when she saw the expression on the face of her patroness.

Still holding her train, Princess Sophie Dorothea raised her free hand and stopped Seramis in her tracks. "My dear Seramis, you must leave!" The princess pushed forward in obvious distress.

Seramis backed away, and almost stumbled into Voltaire, who had just caught up. "Why? What is it, Your Highness?"

"When my brother wrote about your visit, I warned him not to send you!" Princess Sophie Dorothea said, continuing to press Seramis, who had backed into Voltaire, towards the entrance at the far end of the hall.

"We never received a word of it!" Seramis declared.

"I should have expected it, as I knew that I could never influence my brother except in matters of family..." The margravia paused and scanned the room quickly for eavesdroppers. "I had announcements of all new arrivals intercepted—there haven't been many as you can guess—so I could warn you personally! I couldn't trust this message to anyone else!"

"What is it?" Seramis was now leaning close, almost embracing her friend.

Princess Sophie Dorothea leaned closer, whispering, "You must leave now! The king has gone completely—"

"Majesty!" Voltaire shouted as the sounds of marching steps filled the hall. In surprise, Seramis clutched her friend, who straightened and closed her eyes in accepted defeat, sorrow and regret darkening her expression. Servants had thrown open the double doors from which the margravia had surreptitiously entered, and in rushed the monarch, King

Frederick Wilhelm, followed by two of the largest guards Seramis or Voltaire had ever seen.

The Mad King wore bits and pieces of armor which clanked as he entered. He wore greaves over his cavalry boots, and his left hand was gauntleted. Riveted brigandine covered most of his body. The most dangerous aspect of his appearance was not the iron scepter he held in his right hand, but rather the shining gaze that burned beneath his crown. It scolded, it pierced, it blazed at his wife and his diplomatic guests as he walked towards them. His eyes never wavered, fairly glowing in his madness.

While the great ladies curtseyed, Voltaire bowed deeply, saying, "From your loving brother George II of England and Hanover, felicitations on this first day of darkest summer—"

"*Ja! Ja!*" King Frederick Wilhelm bellowed, "*Wer sind Sie? Wer sind Sie alles?*"

"Your Majesty," Princess Sophie Dorothea began—in English, helpfully, and straightening as she spoke, "these are the diplomatic envoys from England that my brother wrote to you about." She indicated Voltaire and Seramis, who remained obeisant during her speech. "They have traveled a great distance to seek your audience concerning the catastrophic weather...." Seeing no change in her husband's comportment and fearing the knife's edge that was his temper, she let her words trail off.

The Mad King simply stared at Voltaire and Seramis as his wife stopped speaking. For the longest time—an eternity to Lady Seramis—he continued to stare, and no one moved, as if in a frozen tableau of the bizarre.

And thus they were, until Voltaire straightened with a flourish and a friendly smile and introduced himself. "I am

Voltaire," he announced. "And this is the Marchioness de Cambridgeshire, Dame Seramis Helleborine, who witnessed firsthand the initial cataclysm the aftermath of which now threatens all of us."

When she was announced by Voltaire, Seramis stood tall, and assumed the same friendly demeanor as he, picking up where he left off. "We have traveled far to—"

"Two? Are you two married?" King Frederick Wilhelm asked of them conversationally, looking from one to the other as if examining the couple. "You're fairly tall!" he exclaimed as he inspected Lady Seramis, who felt increasingly uncomfortable with the king's bald appraisal. Looking Voltaire over, King Frederick Wilhelm pronounced, "You're not! And you're French!"

"My liege," Princess Sophie Dorothea attempted again to start a normal conversation. "He's a poet. We've read some of his work together..."

"A poet?" the Mad King shouted. "A poet! Oh! Did you write this?" He asked and began to sing at the top of his lungs a children's tune while flailing his arms in a lively imitation of a jester.

> "*Au clair de la lune*
> *Mon ami Pierrot*
> *Prête-moi ta plume*
> *Pour écrire un mot...*"

Twirling and dancing, the king was transformed into a spectacle of playfulness. Grabbing a servant, he ran around and around, pulling at the man as he did so, until he let the silent sufferer go to regain his lost composure while the king continued to frantically sing with increasing volume.

"Ma chandelle est morte
Je n'ai plus de feu..."

Stomping and grimacing, the king turned menacing and shouted the rest of the words of the song.

"Ouvre-moi ta porte
Pour l'amour de Dieu!"

Now crying and pleading, he repeated the final lines, inexplicably in English—"For the love of God, Let me in! Open the door!"

Princess Sophie Dorothea started to nonchalantly but physically push Lady Seramis and Voltaire out of the center of the room towards the exit, but was stopped by the king's whispered cries. "Don't go! Please!" His eyes lost their fevered burning, and his entire demeanor changed, becoming supplicating and desperate. "Please... Stay! You can't leave, I command it so!"

Chapter Eight: A Snare

In which our company faces their doom

Despite his ship being overloaded with colonists fleeing the devastation of Virginia, Captain de Ibarra steered *The Agility of Clouds* from Newport into the estuary of the James River before him. Smoke from fires burning in patches throughout the city filled the already cloudy sky. Some fires had been set by those who wished to leave nothing but scorched earth in their wake as they fled: a fiery finish to the work begun by warring factions of militias seeking to take control of the last of the colony's open and functioning ports that was now neither open nor functioning.

"If we can keep to the shallows and the estuaries, we might just see the next morning." It was a mixed message of hope and fear that the captain shouted to the crew and passengers, who filled almost every available space on the *Agility*.

"How will you know when it's morning in this gloom?" White Apple shouted to nobody in particular. In order to seek some distraction from her uncle's paternalistic curiosity, she struggled through the crowd of humanity from one side of the ship to the other, trying to distance herself from Hanaawa while checking the new aerial rudder she had created.

"Did you design all this yourself?" Hanaawa asked, referring to the elaborate mechanism. White Apple continued towards the large cowls covering the blades, pushing her way through the group of frightened and listless refugees.

Quietly, she answered without turning to him, "Yes, Uncle." Upon reaching the port forward propellant, she shouted to the captain, "I advise you to deploy the 'fore propellants." She then reached around a circumferential cowl that not only stabilized the individual blades but also rotated and aimed the force from their operation.

"I very much want to keep us afloat, thank you," he said defensively, dismissing her request.

"They will help." She hopped up to reach the top of the coiled assembly. "Just like the tests," she shouted. Stepping upon the rail, she confirmed the fit of the turning mechanism at the top of the ring.

"Will you please stop going on about it? I know what happened at the tests—I was there." He held the wheel tenderly while the tides flowed around them and out to sea.

"But—" White Apple began.

"White Apple?" Hanaawa interrupted, trying to get his niece's attention.

"What?" White Apple shouted, exasperated. "What is it?" The crew pretended to turn their attention elsewhere. But the majority of the people nearest to White Apple and Hanaawa were refugees, and they gawped openly at the young woman. Ignoring their attention, she stared at Hanaawa in defiance.

"I'm proud of the work you've done. I missed you, but I can see you're busy," he finished lamely. White Apple just stared at him.

She returned to the crow's nest while the crew settled into routine. The refugees barely moved. The night passed by, stifling, oppressive, cold. The fires of Virginia Colony were beyond sight, and the glow on the horizon was far behind them. But ahead was only darkness and uncertainty.

Without White Apple's keen sight, they would have found themselves atop deserted or capsized (but still floating) fishing boats and dhows without warning. More than once she shouted a lookout which raked against everyone's tender nerves like a comb of thorns. Avoiding the flotsam, Captain de Ibarra charted their course using his own reckoning less and less and the instruments more and more. Hours passed, and their slow progress seemed to be the only motion left in the world. Depth markers were called out, the words only to die on the still air.

In a transformation that was missed except upon reflection, a dim light slowly grew in anticipation of a new day. Sadly, only after a fraction of passing time, even the light seemed to give up and settle into a dim grayness that blanketed the coast and the waters around the *Agility*. The day's routine was broken only by the appearance ahead of Chincoteague and the coast that signaled the end of Virginia Colony and the start of the Catholic lands just to the north. Another day's sailing around Cape Hinlopen and past the aptly-named Harbor of Refuge would get them to the late De La Warr's lands and the destination for the refugees.

When they landed on the shore of Delaware, the refugees—laden with their belongings as well as burdens unseen in family left behind and anxieties lurking ahead—slowly made their way down the planks set by the crew. Former Dutch colonists had settled here initially, but the lands had been abandoned for New Amsterdam when the English arrived with their repeated attempts at establishing themselves on this shore. In different times, the land would have welcomed the refugees and rewarded their industry with plenty. But the air was sharp and thin due to the cold, and the refugees turned out to shore in silence with downcast eyes.

Mrs. McClure directed her husband and crew to help the wounded and set up camps and a hospital. The lone caretaker of the estate came upon the scene flustered and red-faced, but was mollified by a mysterious transaction undertaken by Colonel McClure.

"How did you manage that?" Hanaawa asked, watching the man depart.

"It was a simple matter to convince the caretaker that a successful and thriving colony would be the best way to keep the madness in the other colonies from spreading here," the colonel explained. "And as he was an attorney, he also considered some helpful precedents should the will and testament of De La Warr be executed."

"What precedents are those?"

"Gold guineas. I think they were a wise investment from the late baron." The men grinned at one another and set to rounding up the rest of the crew to prepare for departure.

The captain came upon the men, as they boarded the *Agility*. "Where do we sail, sirs?"

"We were sent to learn about Father Time," Hanaawa said. He took his post and helped to stow the planks as they were pulled aboard.

"I think we've learned all we can about him," Mrs. McClure joined in as she arrived. "I know all I ever want to know."

"I wish we would have learned more," White Apple said, to everyone's surprise. Their confusion in turn confused her, as she felt her point was quite obvious. "How are we going to defeat him? Well? Does anyone know?"

"Oh, I don't think you want to trouble yourself with answering that question," came a silky, almost oily voice that slipped into the ear and wrapped itself around a person's most private thoughts without resistance. Father Time materialized into everyone's vision upon the deck of the *Agility* in nearly the exact spot where he had disappeared, a seeming lifetime ago. His arms were crossed over his sunken chest, and he stood nearly a head taller than he had appeared to them all previously. "And you," he said, indicating Mrs. McClure, "I already know all about you, matricide!"

In an inexplicable rage, Mrs. McClure rushed at him, only to be firmly held back by her husband and Hanaawa, with White Apple attempting to throw her arms around them all.

"Gentlemen, look to your leader's weaker half," Father Time said as he pointed at Mrs. McClure. "She will suffer for her insolence. Such a shame that her spirit needs to be crushed!"

Forming a wall between Father Time and his chosen target, Colonel McClure, Hanaawa and Captain de Ibarra stood stone-faced and defiant.

"I can easily go through, around, above, or below each and all of you to get my intended as I wish," Father Time said. And as he spoke, he walked right up to the colonel, except different parts of him moved at different rates, stretching and distorting his body and his features. Father Time's face immediately appeared directly in front of the colonel, while his neck stretched back to the torso several feet behind, seemingly delayed in attempting to catch up with the head. In a flash, he reached for his knife still sheathed at his belt, but

Father Time's hands were there first and flung the weapon away.

"You were always late, you fool!" Father Time said, spitting the words contemptuously. Colonel McClure grappled for Father Time's wrists as the rest of the attacker's body shifted into the same space, finally catching up with his head and hands. But as he reached for Father Time's arms, they twisted away and stretched beyond his reach like unfolding and multiply jointed wings.

With an incoherent shout, Captain de Ibarra pulled his pistol from his belt and slammed the hammer back.

"I can't let you do that, pitiful mercenary," Father Time said coolly as he coiled around himself, as if his top half twisted in anticipation before the rest of him could follow.

Ibarra leveled the flintlock at him, but White Apple jumped between them. "No!" she screamed, and the captain flinched, pulling his weapon up and pointing it away from her.

"Ah, spiny she-demons have taken ye over!" he bellowed, puzzling all as to the nature of his complaint, despite his readily apparent frustration.

"Stop! All of you! He'll kill you if you try!" White Apple pleaded.

"The littlest among you has it right, acquisitor," Father Time said as he uncoiled. One hand shot out and pulled the pistol from Ibarra's grip. As the rest of his body sinuously slid into place after his leading hand, he spoke in a silken whisper to match his arrival, straight into the ear of the captain,

"And so, from hour to hour, we ripe and ripe,
And then, from hour to hour, we rot and rot;
And thereby hangs a tale!"

Laughing, he said, "You will die yet by my hand, I promise!"

"Don't hurt him!" White Apple shouted. "Why are you here? What do you want?" The others were in shock at his appearance and said nothing. Father Time returned to the deck where he had first appeared, walking normally each step of the way.

"You are all so very lucky that I want you alive—with me—right here," Father Time said. Waving his hands vaguely about, he ordered, "Now make this vessel do that thing it does—you know—in the air. Get us above the clouds and I'll tell you what you will do next." Chortling at his conquest, he added, "And if you do it efficiently and without complaint, you will not suffer."

His cruel smile only grew. "Much."

There seemed no end to the corridors and hallways that wound their way through Berliner Schloss. In spite of the expansive staterooms and tall ceilings, its atmosphere was oppressive and claustrophobic, resulting in furtive glances, hushed whispers and a palpable paranoia. Not for the first time in her journeys, Seramis wished she had traveled with her friends to help buoy her spirits. Unfortunately, the repressed local *Mädchen*—their eyes downcast, with their frightened expressions and tremulous hands—depressed Seramis nearly as much as having seen the slaves treated as cargo in Virginia Colony. Her every effort was rebuffed, and every attempt to empathize or offer support was met with stony silence.

When they thought she wasn't listening, Lady Seramis could hear them talking about the king's oversized guards. Apparently, King Frederick Wilhelm had a fascination with giant-sized men. She wasn't sure why the servants attending her were glad that they were short, nor exactly why they feared a term she wasn't familiar with (*begattet*), but it was said to have befallen all of the taller *Mädchen*, who vanished from the palace, their ultimate fate unknown.

When she was finally summoned to court—ostensibly to present her case to the king—Lady Seramis made herself fashionably, if conservatively, presentable. The mood of the Schloss had descended upon her, and she not only missed her friends but also longed for her old study and even her old habits and preferences in a way that suggested that they were not merely gone but gone forever.

When she arrived at the king's apartments, she was confused by the oversized informality of Frederick Wilhelm's court. It seemed more like a hunting lodge grown large, the once-cozy den of a country squire that had somehow expanded in every conceivable dimension. A roaring fire within a massive fireplace large enough for an entire group of even the tallest royal guards blazed with the heat of a burning split tree trunk, while some distance away, the king sat on a throne upon a raised dais covered with carpets and sleeping dogs. When Lady Seramis entered, he stood and shooed away the dogs, ordering his guards to move the dais a bit closer to the fire. As he pushed his way through the great hunting hounds who wanted only to return to their warm spots (made more attractive now that they were nearer to the fireplace), King Frederick Wilhelm invited her to sit in a chair on the floor just off of the dais.

"*Bitte! Setzen sie auf,*" he said, then waved away his ill manners. "What am I saying? You are English, *Ja?* Will you sit? My Sophie Dorothea's brother sits on the English throne, so we are all friends here? *Ja?* We are friends?" The king's eyes fairly shone with his questions, reflecting the crackling blaze in the fireplace. Lady Seramis curtseyed before quietly taking the proffered seat. She casually wondered where Voltaire was, and wished Princess Sophie Dorothea was here.

Lady Seramis replied solemnly, "My visit to you, your Majesty, comes at a most grave time—"

"Stop the serious talk. We are friends, *Ja?* Don't talk like a man—I can only once forgive your off... trans... er, your... *Verstoß? Beleidigung?*"

"Offense?" offered Seramis, who couldn't help but raise an eyebrow at the suggestion.

"Ja!" the king bellowed, throwing up his hands in delight, before noticing her expression. "What is that look?" His eyes narrowing with suspicion, he leaned forward on his throne.

"Sire?" Seramis naturally resumed a neutral expression of slight surprise.

"Ah! That is much better." the king said joyously and leaned back. "*Sehr gut!* Women should look just like that. And sound like that, too."

With the lightning change in his mood, he slapped the arms of the chair with his palms. "But *Mädchen* should not talk about seriousness. So, why did my brother England send you?" he asked rhetorically.

"Perhaps Your Majesty would wish that both my partner and I were to—"

"That other?" the king interrupted. "He is your... partner?" His head tilted, as if his neck muscles were contracting. "Are you married?"

"I believe, sire, that—regarding marriage—questions of timing and inclination would need to be answered before—"

"Ach! Do not speak that way!" he said, putting his hands to his ears, his eyes widening as if in pain, while the rest of his features contorted into a grimace of inconceivable cruelty.

"*Meine Liebchen!*" came a cry from the doorway; it sounded like Princess Sophie Dorothea to Lady Seramis, but her eyes were locked upon the king out of fear of what he might do. However, at the sound of his wife's voice, his expression softened, and he began to weep, covering his face as sobs burst from within. As Princess Sophie Dorothea rushed to his side Seramis made to rise from her seat but was kept there by a gesture from the princess, who cooed at her husband while cradling his head to her bosom. Speaking in German, she told him that Seramis was a talented musician, but that artists and musicians can't be expected to live like the rest of us—at least, such is what Seramis understood of what Princess Sophie Dorothea said as she murmured soothingly to the distraught monarch.

Lady Seramis stood when Voltaire arrived, having been summoned by the princess after rumors of the court interview had reached her. The king had begun to recover as his wife talked about their son's wedding on the morrow, and he further started to invent a fantasy about how King George II of England had kindly sent two ambassadors—but she never got any further.

"Who are to be married at the same time as our Fritz!" the king said in English, jumping up from his wife's embrace and walking over to Voltaire and Lady Seramis.

"*Nein, Liebchen!*" shouted Princess Sophie Dorothea. But she was waved away by the king who grabbed both Voltaire and Lady Seramis.

Voltaire tried to demur, saying, "Your Majesty, no—"

"I insist!" shouted King Frederick Wilhelm.

"Please, sire, I beg of you—" said Seramis. The king's grip began to tighten on her arm, and she hushed in surprise.

Taking this as an affirmation, the mad king bellowed "*Sehr gut!*" as he thrust the hands of Voltaire and Lady Seramis together. "Tomorrow will be such a lovely—how do you say? Ceremony!"

The Fury of Storms

Seramis took the news of her impending nuptials in good humor, as she felt she had been threatened with worse than mere marriage in the past. Being forced into participating in a ceremony made absolutely no sense—wasn't marriage a contract, and simply null and void without her consent? It was all just a ritual, and had no bearing on how she felt about Voltaire or about anything else for that matter.

Seramis was soon surprised, however, at the ruthless efficiency of her handlers. She was measured from head to toe, weighed, bathed, washed, and powdered. When it was over, Seramis felt empty but with a growing sense of having been violated, and she broke down in tears.

As it turned out, she wasn't the only bride-to-be sobbing that evening. But the next morning, the complex preparations for the wedding rivaled any military campaign she had ever witnessed, making the previous day's ministrations seem like a lazy stroll along a country lane. In a blur that left no time for emotions of any kind, Lady Seramis was made to look every inch a princess, and was eventually hustled to a carriage and a very short trip to the cathedral next to the Berliner Schloss.

Marched past thousands of guests (none of whom appeared to be nobility, but were instead seemingly well-dressed commoners), Seramis and the bride for Frederick Wilhelm II, or 'Fritz' as he was called by friends and family, were the very picture of resplendent passivity when they arrived to kneel at the altar within the Berliner Dom. She hadn't even time enough to learn the name of the other bride, although for the other's sake she hoped that the prince's mind was in better shape than the king's.

An expectant atmosphere filled the cathedral, oppressive in its own way, yet entirely different from the mood in the palace. Whispers of the expected arrival of gifts for the guests floated to Lady Seramis as the ministers chanted the celebration prayer. Lady Seramis tried to occupy her mind with abstractions as she knelt, but focus was impossible. Where was Voltaire, at present? She tried unsuccessfully to stay still with her hands folded upon her breast as she was instructed, but her knees began to complain. She surreptitiously glanced to the thrones on her right and saw the king and Princess Sophie Dorothea. They, too, fidgeted as they sat. It seemed to Lady Seramis that the prayers and stories were being repeated, while she and the bride waited.

Let's finish this. Where's Voltaire?

An officer in the Prussian Cavalry (to judge by his uniform and boots, Seramis thought) made his way to the monarch as if he had somehow materialized behind the throne. She had heard nothing, and the officer stopped at attention as if he had been there the entire time. Seramis thought that not even the king had noticed, when he nearly jumped as the officer leaned forward to discreetly whisper in his ear. Princess Sophie Dorothea, sitting next to the king, was plainly listening, despite pretending not to, as she stiffened in her seat and clutched the fan she was holding in surprise or fear.

The officer either repeated or further embellished his pronouncement, as the king listened without moving for some time. It was clear that the officer had stopped speaking, but he remained standing, waiting for confirmation or further instructions. Princess Sophie Dorothea looked at Lady Seramis, who dared to look openly and questioningly back at her friend and patron. The ministers were about to restart the ceremony again as the officer resumed speaking, only to be interrupted by a scream of inarticulate rage. The king leaped to his feet and shouted *"Was ist das?"* to the surprise of all, eliciting a gasp from the assembly.

Princess Sophie Dorothea waved to her attendants who stepped forth from in front of the pews and walked to the center aisle. Announcing that the giving of gifts would now commence, she had seemingly taken charge. Frederick Wilhelm continued to yell in German as Seramis stood— painfully and slowly, as her legs had gone to sleep while she was kneeling—and looked at her friend directly.

"You! *Was hast du mit meinem Sohn gemacht?*" the king shouted at Seramis, drawing out the last word as if vocalized by pure anguish alone. "What have you done with my son?" he repeated in English. As he moved toward Seramis, her attention shifted and she noticed that the officer was no longer there. Distracted by the realization (and the seeming threat from the monarch), Seramis jumped when Princess Sophie Dorothea grabbed her by the arm.

"You must get out of here!" the margravia said, as she pulled the jilted Seramis away from the altar. They pushed past the row of guards who had lined up behind the attendants carrying bags of coins. "Come with me!" she cried as she plunged into the crowd spilling into the central aisle from the pews where they had sat during the interrupted ceremony.

Seramis followed behind her friend, befuddled. "What happened?"

Waving her hands in front of her, Princess Sophie Dorothea parted the crowd as they rushed to form lines to receive their coins. Those nearest began to kneel on the floor in obeisance and would have slowed them down, but for the margravia shouting "Out of the way!" Turning to Seramis, she said, "Voltaire and Fritz have escaped just this morning, before the wedding!"

"What?" Seramis said. *I've been left alone at a wedding that I didn't even want?* She was both incensed and overjoyed at the turn of events, whereupon she spied a hint of gray daylight in the massive open doors just ahead looking like an exit to this mad dream.

"I'm so sorry, dear Seramis," Princess Sophie Dorothea said. "I wish you would have never come here! All the nobles have left, and you should have stayed away, too! They faced the same fate: if unmarried, a forced marriage, to be followed by giving away gifts to the common people whether newly married or not."

"That explains the exodus I witnessed," Lady Seramis said.

"I don't know what possessed the king to force his ideas upon you and Voltaire. But he grows more disturbed every day. I fear for your safety, so you must leave, too."

The princess and Lady Seramis were now past the crowd, and about to exit the cathedral, when the same officer who had earlier brought the news to the king stepped in front of the open door, blocking their route to freedom.

"Out of my way, General von Schwerin!" commanded the margravia.

"Of course," the general replied in smooth, cultured English as he took a bold step directly in front of Seramis. "The king commands that you leave the girl, Your Highness."

Princess Sophie Dorothea pulled Seramis behind her and faced the general, who continued to step to the side, as if to bypass her and reach his target. "I command that you allow me to pass, unmolested," she said.

"Of course," the general said, smiling and still stepping to the side, circling farther around the pair. "And further you shall also be unencumbered. Allow me to help you divest yourself of your burden." The princess and marchioness were completely turned around now, facing towards the altar. Princess Sophie Dorothea stepped backwards while pushing Seramis behind her in the direction of the exit. However, the king's giant guards, having just entered the cathedral through the door, boxed in Seramis from behind and took her away, lifting her to their shoulders unceremoniously and exiting just as they had arrived.

"Stop!" cried the princess ineffectively, as she turned and tears flowed down her face.

Smirking, the general spoke in mock sympathy. "I know, I know. Do you always cry at weddings, too?" Laughing, he followed the guards carrying Seramis out of the cathedral and back to the palace.

Chapter Nine: A Disaster

In which there is a most distressing tragedy

"Do we do as he says?" Captain de Ibarra piloted the *Agility* out of the foggy shallows and into Delaware Bay, keeping an eye on both the open waters around him and the menacing figure of Father Time. While the currents shifted continuously, the shape that stood on the main deck remained frozen in place as the crew went out of their way to avoid him.

"I don't know," Hanaawa whispered, perplexed. "What does he want?"

Mrs. McClure looked sheepish and spoke hesitantly. "I'm sorry for... for losing my..."

"It's all right." Colonel McClure's worried smile, meant to reassure her, never reached his eyes.. He looked back to the captain. "If we sound a general alarm, the entire crew would join us—"

"From what we just saw," Ibarra whispered, "we wouldn't lay a finger on him and we would lose everything."

"I think if he wanted us dead we would already be so," Mrs. McClure said. "Especially after my outburst. He must need us for something."

"We need him," White Apple asserted as she leaned forward, emphatic.

"Wh—? I'm not forgetting ye jus' done me some good. But if ye keep spouting nonsense, I'll decommission ye!"

"Nonsense? Did you see what he did? We need to find out who or what made him into that! Do you think he just picked that up on his own?" Her whisper grew louder, perchance attracting attentions better left elsewhere.

"White Apple"—Hanaawa nearly shouted, and quickly lowered his voice—"is right. We were asked by Lady Seramis—although that was a long time ago, and a lot has happened since—to find out about this creature. This is our chance."

Expecting more recriminations and scolding, White Apple was surprised to hear him take her side. She wondered at her own doubts of him, as she thought about how he'd always supported her, and tears started flowing. Stoically, she kept silent, however, and let the tears roll down her cheeks, while forcing her breathing to be even. While she focused on her own composure, some small part of her was able to be aware of Father Time as an entity. Nothing more—just an awareness—maybe it was imagined? Distracted by the sense, she tried to focus upon the entity, to try to determine more than just the vague identity she perceived, but when she tried to focus upon the concept, the sensation slipped away.

"Let's get started, then," the captain said without looking directly at her, and speaking louder so that all could hear. "White Apple, take charge of the aerial rudder."

"Aye," she said, grateful for the task and with a growing eagerness to see her invention at work.

"Bosun, call stations!" the captain said. Crew scrambled into the rigging to ready the gas envelopes. Colonel and Mrs. McClure avoided the center of the main deck as they went to their watch position at the bow together.

"I don't know what to feel, Cy!" Mrs. McClure whispered. "Are we really going into the air?"

"I haven't a clue, dear Sarah," her husband said. "But I'm glad we're together, whatever happens!" He lashed himself and his perplexed wife to the rail as he'd been instructed. "See? We stay together, like it or not!"

"Bosun, take the wheel! I'm going to get this ship aloft!" Ibarra took his place at the controls for the pitchblende gas as Hanaawa returned to the main deck to keep an eye on Father Time. "Ready and steady!" the captain shouted. "Stations! Report!" White Apple announced "ready" as did the lookout and the crew in the rigging.

The entire ship was still, matching the specter who stood unspeaking and seemingly unconcerned about the activity around him.

With grim determination, the captain shouted as he turned the lever on the pitchblende. "Deploy main envelope!" The crew cast off the lashes, and gas began to fill the giant canvas bags. "Deploy aerial rudder to vertical, quarter speed!" White Apple threw the levers with both hands, and the cowled propellants lifted from the deck as the arms that held them swung up and away from its center until they passed vertical and came to rest about sixty degrees directly away from the ship. "Keep us level, White Apple!"

"First team!" White Apple called out to the rowers. The arms of the oars were connected to freewheeling gears that drove the blades of the propellants. "Brevis!" One fourth of the rowers started a slow count, pulling on the oars on the count of every 'four', thus starting the blades in all of the cowls to spin.

"Amazing!" Hanaawa shouted. White Apple looked back at him and smiled.

Captain de Ibarra barked "Focus!" as he opened the gas valves farther. "Ready for main envelopes: full!" The two main envelopes that ran longer than the length of the ship and were attached to the central spars and the main rigging continued filling with the pitchblende gas and started to pull upwards upon the ship. "Aerial rudder: half speed!" As the propellants responded, the ship stopped being skittish upon its keel and rose up steadily.

"Oh!" Mrs. McClure gasped as she watched the water slowly fall away.

"Get ready for this then," Ibarra shouted. "Deploy secondary envelopes! Maximum buoyancy! Deploy aerial rudder for full lift!"

"Aye!" White Apple said, and pushed the levers to their maximum, dropping the cowls to the waterline of the floating craft. "Full position!" she shouted. At this position and speed, they stabilized the craft as it rode the headwinds from the land out to sea.

As he filled them with gas, Captain de Ibarra watched the secondary envelopes carefully as they expanded, tapering to points and raking towards the aft. The water dropped away below them as they floated up and away from the Earth. Into the sky the crew and passengers soared, getting soaked and drenched by the clouds settling away from them until they shivered.

Just as it became nearly intolerable, and the clouds seemed to go on without end, they broke free of them and rose above the cover. For the first time since the column at Bermuda had exploded, the crew of the *Agility* could see sunlight. Blinding light flooded White Apple's vision as she and the rest gasped at the sight.

The captain leveled off their ascent and cheered, "Full on! Here's to the best crew on sea or cloud!"

"Hurrah!" the crew chorused. Their response was muted at the reason for their latest ascent, but the performance had been cheer-worthy, regardless.

They had just pulled into a strong trade wind that pulled at the sails, straining steady at fifteen knots according to the instruments. At this altitude and speed, the wind was deafening and constant. Captain de Ibarra took a reading of the sun and set the chronometer, while the rest of the crew waited. When the captain finished, he, too, stopped and waited. There was no conversation, no movement, no one said or did anything.

The silence held for a few minutes before Father Time said, "What?" Glancing around he saw that everyone was looking at him. "Oh, yes. Right. You're waiting on me to tell you what to do. How very fitting, you know, as I do truly lord over you all." As if claiming ownership of the vistas surrounding them, he spread his arms wide. "I brought you here!" Laughing inexplicably, he continued, "Well, yes. I commanded you to get this thing into the air—but before that! I manipulated everything that happened..." When the crew remained silent, he dropped his arms and the smile left his face. "Yes, you get the point. Why do I bother?"

Captain de Ibarra's voice was ice. "You said you'd tell us where to go?"

White Apple unlashed herself from her station and made her way back to the aft quarterdeck in silence. Father Time smiled, beatifically unaware as she maneuvered into position.

The Fury of Storms

His eyes closed, Tempus spoke as if in a trance. "I can see—yes. Yes, I can... I can see that you're going to be difficult, Captain." He didn't move. "I promised you would die, and I think I need to set an example..." So swiftly that none could follow, Father Time spun around and, like a coiled snake, launched himself at Captain de Ibarra. But at the last possible moment, he stopped himself short as his path had been blocked.

White Apple was standing in front of the captain, her arms crossed on her chest.

"H-h-how?" Incredulity grabbed his voice and only reluctantly let it go.

White Apple simply stared at him, proud and defiant. Father Time stood tall, looking down at the mere child in front of him. He crossed his arms in mocking imitation of the child.

"Could it be, perhaps? An apprentice with some talent, maybe?

"To Ireland, for now." Father Time spoke to Captain de Ibarra above White Apple's head while still staring at her. "See if you can get this thing to Ireland, and make it quick. I'm already there," he added cryptically, "and I hate to wait."

Captain de Ibarra's charts weren't as detailed with regards to the North Atlantic as he would have liked had he been sailing. But floating above the storms (for the most part) on the trade winds above the Gulf Stream and North Atlantic Current meant that he had some leeway, so to speak. Or as he put it, "Some latitude due to the altitude."

But the altitude wasn't to stay, as Father Time ordered the *Agility* to go beneath the cloud ceiling, or about one thousand feet above the surface of the North Atlantic. At once, they came upon what appeared to be a giant waterspout as viewed from a distance, but upon closer examination was revealed to a living sculpture made of water in the shape of Father Time. Literally standing off of the coast of Ireland, the jets and sprays of the water lent a softer finish to what otherwise was a harsh and severe representation—one that delighted the subject, apparently—as Father Time shouted to it, "Show me the way!"

To the crew's astonishment, the sculpture raised its left arm and pointed inland. In response to the gesture, "Can you follow a simple direction?" Father Time taunted the Captain.

"Can you fall off the side of me ship?" the Captain answered grimly.

This was ignored, however, as White Apple asked Father Time a question. "You were not in control of that apparition, were you?"

"What is it to you, weak one?" Father Time retorted. "And why couldn't I be? I can control all creation itself."

"You were in sympathetic contact, like tapping into a great potential power," White Apple said. "You framed a question, and the source of the power itself answered you."

"Why are you troubling me with this? Do you wish to die?" Father Time asked rhetorically.

"Because, first—in general—I'm beginning to get a hint at what it is you're seeking," White Apple answered. "And, second—specifically—no, I most definitely do not want to die."

Floating over Ireland, Father Time ordered, "Bring us down—safely—in that valley."

"Do you wish me to just drop the ship upon the land?" asked Captain de Ibarra. The days of sunshine hadn't improved his mood. And now, once again in the perpetual twilight and gloom of the cloud cover, his mood matched the setting.

"Find a lake or whatever it is you must," Father Time said.

Pulling out his eyeglass, the captain protested. "The lakes are all frozen in that gap!"

White Apple had been eyeing the land a bit farther on. "There's a larger lake that still has some open water just a few leagues to the east!"

"You're being useful, pixie!" Tempus's compliment was most unusual and thereby drew nearly everyone's attention.

Ignoring him, White Apple continued. "There appears to be a town just beyond."

Father Time's words thundered, "Make certain that none of them spy us, if you want them to live. I will brook no delay, and will rid myself of the entire population of pitiful 'townsfolk' without hesitation!"

The successful surfacing of the *Agility* into open water free from ice was entirely due to the new aerial rudder, which kept them in place while the buoyant gas was vented from the giant envelopes. The crew pounded away the ice from the secondary envelopes as they were furled, and the ship touched down.

"Which way?" shouted Father Time to the elements around him. In answer, lightning traversed the clouds back towards the gap that they had just flown over. He called out, "Little ignorant one, would you like to gain some inkling of what real power is?" The crew froze at the tone of that invitation; the danger and challenge in the words were palpable, but White Apple strode forward confidently, shaking off the protective gesture from her uncle.

Hanaawa whispered a plaintive inquiry, unacknowledged and unheeded.

For the rest of the day, Lady Seramis had only the company of Major General Kurt Christoph von Schwerin, with questions alternating between her past and her involvement in the *affaire d'espionnage* that had liberated Fritz from his father's madness. Lady Seramis maintained complete nonchalance, now hiding her elation at her own freedom from an imposed marriage, then hiding her despair at being imprisoned. Or did she feel a twinge of sorrow over something else? While she had never contemplated the specifics of marriage, she had at times imagined herself in a wedding ceremony—but never one where she was left at the altar, jilted by her groom. In the space between the questions that she easily answered—in fact, mostly by not answering directly the questions put forth by the general—she realized she was surprised that her 'partner' had left without her. But immediately upon thinking that she had been abandoned, she held out hope that Voltaire was just around the corner, having planned on this turn of events—her imprisonment— and furthermore her eventual rescue.

Her interrogator, Schwerin, left and returned many times during the day. When he returned for the final time, he appeared to be genuinely sad. "In the morning, your trial and sentence will commence..."

"Your judicial system seems to take certain precedents for granted, General," Lady Seramis said.

He didn't rise to the bait. "It is very efficient, yes," he said sadly. "But I can reassure you that your part in the treason that has been perpetrated against the person of His Most Excellent Majesty has not been sufficiently proven. Your confederate, however, will be tried and sentenced to death in absentia..."

"Are you sad that I shall keep my head?" Lady Seramis asked lightly of the general.

"Oh no, Lady," he said, removing his tricorn, "but I am heartbroken—that for the crime of assisting you my princess, the lovely and true Sophie Dorothea, must lose hers!"

Simply not believing the news that her friend and patron, the Princess Sophie Dorothea, would die in the morning, Seramis felt confident that such a harsh fate would be ultimately averted. Her confidence was shallow, however, as she tossed and turned the entire night; the servants assigned to her found her sitting alone in her bed the next morning, shaken and distraught.

Passively, Seramis let herself be clothed in a plain dress while the wan light of dawn made a tepid showing before being hidden by heavy clouds. In Voltaire's absence, she thought that she should start planning her escape and the rescue of her friend. But every avenue seemed to be blocked. The servants could only leave one at a time in a complicated arrangement where a handful of guards, with swords drawn, enter the room—leaving their like number just outside the single door in each direction.

Before she herself was allowed to leave the room, Lady Seramis's wrists were shackled by heavy iron fetters that cut into her hands, which were then chained together and held by two guards at either side. She wondered at the extreme security measures that had been taken; could they be typical?

Or, was she being afforded some extraordinary restraint specifically for some perceived threat of escape? The irons dragged at her already strained emotions, leaving her to meekly and passively follow her captors.

"Please," she asked silently to herself, "if there be any justice—or a spark of chivalry anywhere—do not allow this travesty to continue!" Walking through the courtyard, she looked to the skies. Soldiers lined the yard, and a rescue seemed out of the question, even if the *Agility*, leading an entire squadron of like craft, were to suddenly burst forth from the clouds.

As she was pushed into a windowless and iron-reinforced coach, Lady Seramis looked in vain for Princess Sophia Dorothea, both to provide whatever spark of hope she could to any who might see her and to glean some small optimism from just a view of her friend. The ride to the court was a short one, although the journey took her off of the island where the Berliner Schloss und Dom were located. Upon her arrival at her destination, Lady Seramis finally saw the princess across from her in the chambers and separated from her by dozens of soldiers. She casually noted that the entire assembly consisted of older, pale men in dark robes, and that she and the margravia—the condemned—were the only women in attendance.

With an involuntary cry, Lady Seramis recovered her spirit and struggled briefly against her captors. A handful of soldiers pushed her back into a bench and cruelly gagged her, silencing her pleas as she was held in place. Princess Sophia Dorothea looked up once at the cry from her friend, then cast her gaze to the floor, on which it remained focused.

The 'Blood Court' was declared to be in session, accompanied by a lengthy pronouncement of the enlightened nature of justice as demonstrated by the recent abolition of torture as a sentence by law within the last decade. This was followed by a representative of the Lutheran Church blessing the proceedings, underscoring the fact that capital punishment was not expressly forbidden in scripture. The king appeared and nodded his approval before sitting down (his only contribution to the process).

Princess Sophie Dorothea was summarily convicted of treason—along with the crown prince and Voltaire, in absentia. Merely mentioned in passing, the commoners implicated in the plot had already been executed. For subverting the customs of the kingdom and for attempting to spirit away the captive bride, the princess was condemned to death and Lady Seramis condemned to watch.

It was a cruel and entirely needless act, and Seramis wished her tears to obscure her vision, her anguish to blot out the sound. She swore that the death of so great a lady would eventually lead not just to revenge for revenge's sake, but to the form of vengeance in which justice for all would prevail. She cried as the princess kneeled before a stained block. The guards held Lady Seramis's head in place, so that even if she wished to turn away, she would be unable. The executioner raised his axe. There were no spoken commands, no audible signals to warn the condemned before the axe fell, and Seramis fervently hoped that her friend's death was swift and painless. Through the gag in her mouth Seramis cried out in despair, a howl that started deep in her chest, and filled her entire being without relenting until she collapsed.

The Fury of Storms

Chapter Ten: A Foreboding

In which paths are chosen and new alliances formed

Lady Seramis was carried to her cell and dumped unceremoniously, left to dream as she slept. In her dreams, she relived the experience of being bound and gagged and witnessing the death of her friend, the Princess Sophie Dorothea. But as the blade fell and as Lady Seramis began to howl in pain, she grew in size as she had once witnessed Father Time grow. And like him, she became more immaterial as she expanded to nearly touch the high ceiling of the Blood Court with her head, and the gags and fetters fell away from her like so many dead leaves from a tree in winter. But she was too late, and her friend and benefactor who had been like a mother to her died in this dream just as she had died while Seramis was awake.

But in her dream, a hissing sound tore at her eardrums, and she somehow snatched away every weapon from every astonished onlooker as if they had become mesmerically or magnetically under her power. Without trying, she pulled them from hands and holsters, sheaths and scabbards. Soon, although she herself was yet immaterial, she had become shrouded entirely in weapons from head to toe, halberds and pikes armoring her legs, muskets and pistols covering her trunk. Her arms bristled with the swords and daggers of everyone present, including the executioner's bloody axe. In terror, the denizens of the court screamed and fled from

Seramis's transformation into a towering leviathan of death. Enraged at the execution of her friend, she screamed and tore about her, kicking, punching, clubbing about her in a mass carnage that left herself weeping and bloody.

She awoke from such a dream completely exhausted, yet filled with burning anger at the injustice that had been perpetrated in the name of a clearly insane monarch. However, as she opened her eyes, she saw General von Schwerin in her cell, sitting stone-faced upon a stool while holding his white leather gloves. "What are you...?" she managed to croak before he waved her question away with his gloves.

"I am here to transport you to your quarters in the palace, where you will be confined under house arrest." Disappointment fairly dripped from his words. "I had a glimmer of hope that your earlier arrest for witchcraft—yes, I have my spies as well and they hinted at powers you might wield—was not merely a political farce. Evidently it was, much to my sorrow, unless you clearly chose to be powerless and wanted to see your friend die in front of you."

Seramis jumped out of bed and screamed at him as he sat unflinching. "You! If I could shoot my burning eyes at you and that lunatic you call king, I would wish that I were a witch!" She could feel a pathway open up before her as she raged, a pathway of bloody vengeance and terrible power. Schwerin swiftly moved as if to strike her across the face with his gloves but froze at her changing expression.

She froze, standing tall in furious and righteous anger. "I am who I choose to be," she said. "Not what you see in me." Her white-hot fury cooled into a tempered steel of calculation and planning. She had swiftly chosen a different path, one that might not only ultimately avenge Princess Sophie Dorothea but also—if she were successful—reshape the destiny of Europe, perhaps even the world.

He marveled at the coolness and calm in her transformed features, and was torn between the futile expression of dominance in slapping her—which he now felt would never break her to his will—and his own calculated study of what she might be plotting, even in her downfall. He erred on the side of temperance, and knocked once upon the door. Unlike the previous day, there was no host of guards. Only two maids entered with boots and a cowled cape for Lady Seramis to wear as she was taken back to the Berliner Schloss.

Lady Seramis's transfer to the castle was uneventful, and the general immediately left her alone in her room upon their arrival. The dark clouds outside were no match for the foul mood and dank, oppressive spirit imparted upon the palace. Alone, Seramis could feel the call to action belatedly fill her. She had been acquiescent and complicit, but that was no longer the case.

The coach that had taken Voltaire and her across Europe had been emptied of its things, including her gowns and even the cosmetics case and the wig holder, which now appeared in her room. Using these items, Seramis proceeded to fashion an effigy of herself. She then proceeded to hang it from the beams along the ceiling so that she could try to fool—if only for a moment, for that was all she needed—an onlooker into believing that she had killed herself in her despair.

When one of the maids entered while Seramis hid behind the door, the resulting scream announced that the figure had accomplished its goal. As the lone guard burst in from the hallway, Seramis swiftly tripped him from behind and, picking up his musket, clubbed him in the head before tossing the weapon away. Dressed once again entirely in black, Seramis placed a finger upon the lips of the maid to silence her before binding and gagging her with her own apron. Apologizing to the maid as she left, she closed the door to her room and silently stole away to the streets of Berlin.

Using a diverse multitude of identities and routes, Seramis made her way to the Hanoverian Lands controlled by the British monarch, George II. Arriving in Bremen dressed as a peasant carrying an innocent-looking trundle, Seramis happened upon a group of officers, of mixed company according to their standards and flags, one of which she thought she recognized. Setting the tub on the road in front of her and holding her arms upright, she stood directly in the path of one of the cantering horses.

Coming to a stop directly in front of her, the rider called out, "I've no metal but steel for my enemies, and not a coin to be had for alms!"

"But can you spare a greeting for an old friend?" Lady Seramis spoke in an affected, ragged voice while straightening and pulling the cowl back from her head.

"By Gods' teeth! What is this?" the rider called out, removing his bicorn as the other officers on horseback gathered round.

"I think I answered that already!" she replied in her natural voice, as she confirmed the identity of the rider. "And if you can't spare a greeting for an old friend, perhaps you could lend me some steel and we'll face our enemies together!" She removed the shawl that she had pulled up around her face and pulled two flintlock pistols from the tub. "I'll take arms by your side in defense of our king—although I should think to learn how to properly use these first!"

"Oh, sweet mercy!" Albion cried and jumped down from his horse. "I never thought I'd see you again! Your appearance here is both miraculous and yet perfectly suited to your talents!" He pulled Seramis into his arms, and they embraced while the other officers looked askance, wondering at the unusual display of familiarity—until they remembered discretion and pretended to be interested in passing carts and various components of local architecture.

"I was hoping against hope that I'd find you," Seramis said. "I gathered from sources in Hamburg said that you'd be here, personally overseeing the evacuation of ambassadors recalled in the wake of disintegrating relations."

"Indeed!" he said in fierce humor. "The king's sister lies dead and yet, we only talk of 'relations' when English blood boils for war and vengeance!"

"I was there, Henry—they forced me to watch..." She choked on the memory. "She was my friend and a savior too kind for words..."

"Then what I've heard is true!" Henry fell to his knees. "Forgive me for my rushed and callous words!" The rest of the officers removed their hats and helms.

"You're forgiven as by your pure heart there was never one so true! And let us steel ourselves, and cleanse these lands by arms if diplomacy fails!"

Rising, he agreed. "Let no intention be more clear than our hunger for justice!" Waving his bicorn above his head, Albion joined the officers in thrusting their headgear upward and shouting their approval, cheering for a simple woman in simple dress promising a common aim.

Father Time led White Apple across the ice to an island called Innisfallen, the significance of which he explained to the young follower at great length and with high oratory. White Apple only half-listened and was caught short when he asked, "What do you see? Or are you as blind as the rest?"

"What?" White Apple stalled for time and chafed under his boorishness.

"Are you deaf as well as blind?" he chided. "Look around you, and if you have half the sight you pretend, tell me what you see!"

She glared at him, but stopped at the edge of the island and looked about. At first, all she could see were the wind-tossed fir trees shedding their dusting of snow, although it was all a bit hazy—there was no fog at present. She stepped a few paces to the right and saw that she had been standing in a tunnel of dim light, Now that she had stepped out of it, she could see that it made its way up the shore of the island in one direction, while heading straight away in the other.

Father Time laughed at his own private joke, a cruel humor that revealed itself only to him. White Apple ignored the hateful mirth, and saw that there were more tunnels of light leading in several directions, and that a few of them converged here upon this island. "These lines? What are they?" White Apple asked.

"I ask you to look around you, and all you see are lines?" He laughed dismissively as he walked up to her. "What use are you? Can't you see what's all around you?"

"Do you mean them?" She snapped in frustration, pointing at bent figures shambling out of the forest upon the island, quickly heading straight towards them with malicious intent.

Father Time laughed. "Finally!" Quoting the Bard, he said,

"What they are,
Yet I know not:
But they shall be
The terrors of the earth!"

He continued to laugh as rough hands seized both him and White Apple, bodily lifted them up, and carried them towards the convergence of the lines of power.

The figures represented humanity in all its many shapes and forms, in that they were, to each and every one, uniquely formed or twisted in shape. One, missing a leg, used a crutch to make its way; others, missing both legs, pulled themselves along the rough ground; for those missing one arm, the other arm did double duty; if missing both arms, the figure made up for the lack in vicious cries and shrieks. But mere physical deformity was not the sole hideousness of this band—such were merely the vagaries of life. Their twisted, evil souls held only hate, and it was that hate which Father Time cultivated here and throughout Europe. These few had been herded by Father Time's malice along lines unseen and unfelt to the small hillock atop the island of Innisfallen and had practiced cruel rituals and sacrifices upon unwary travelers or upon their own number as well. And they were in the midst of a sacrifice, yet without a victim. Until now.

White Apple was nonplussed, as she feared for her life but also wondered at the passivity of Father Time, who had previously warped portions of himself in and out of synchronized time and handily bested three able-bodied fighters. But here, where not a handful among the hundreds of cackling and brutish figures could be considered the physical equal of the average person, he had been easily caught and was now borne to a clearing where two tunnels of light converged.

At the edge of the clearing White Apple was tied to a tree by the clumsy, shambling creatures. Father Time was hung upside-down upon an improvised crucifix at the center, laughing all the while. While the knots binding her were tight if ill-formed, the ones that bound him to the rough-hewn wood cut into his flesh, bringing forth from within him not blood but instead a foul ichor with the visible consistency of black tar.

Screams and shrieks filled the air, and White Apple wondered if the crew of the *Agility* heard them, too, and might soon be here. When—or if—they arrived, what might they think of this? For her part, she had little time to think, as the crowd grew violent; they crudely jostled and pushed against each other as each vied to be close to the intended sacrifice. One, larger than the rest, howled and brandished a cruelly curved knife. Pushing aside the others who were between itself and the victim, it brandished the blade above Father Time's bare throat.

White Apple meant to scream in defiance, but she stopped before she could begin. Why stop this mad proceeding? Although she thought surely she would be sacrificed afterwards, she wondered whether she should protest the murder of a single horror, or by allowing this crime, somehow prevent a world engulfed in horrors. But the sight that transpired before her stirred revulsion and nausea, and a brief cry erupted from her lips as the blade tore through Father Time's throat, leaving a jagged second grin where it cut.

Instead of blood, a noxious gas poured forth from the gaping wound, as if a fetid and bloated corpse had been pierced. The gas immediately caused retching and convulsions among those closest to the sacrifice, leaving those still mobile to claw and scramble away from the victim to the woods for shelter. None made it, however, as the gas spread and slew all it touched. White Apple stared transfixed as she struggled to free herself from the ropes. The gas, glowing a sickly green from the light emanating from the ghostly tunnels that converged upon the clearing, crept towards her as she twisted violently against her bonds.

When the gas reached White Apple, a heartfelt good-bye fell from her lips. But instead of death, she found freedom. Her bonds dissolved and the gas dissipated. Stumbling forward, she stopped short of stepping upon one of the many lifeless, contorted bodies that now littered the ground, staring back at her with unseeing eyes in frozen expressions. She almost started to run, but turned out of a morbid curiosity to look upon the slain Father Time, who appeared to stare back at her, still smiling out of twin grins. In shock, she watched as he kicked forward and pulled himself out of his bonds as if they hadn't existed. Turning towards White Apple, he jerked his head to each side with a loud crack and grinned from a single, evil smile, his wounds disappearing even as she watched.

"Congratulations, initiate." His voice was cold and uninviting. "I was originally intent upon raising a local army, but it appears that I've found something better: an apprentice!" Father Time's eyes glowed at his personal triumph. "Within Hell's Heart we join in partnership!"

Unbidden, words came to White Apple from centuries past, remembered from a rare book containing the story of a traveler on the edge of the underworld...

"O miserable me! how I did shudder
When he seized on me!"

Upon their return, White Apple was greeted with cheers from the crew of the Agility, while Father Time was ignominiously ignored. She returned the cheers with a hooded expression that was also ignored, but in this case out of politeness. White Apple was left with the fear and confusion from the implications of what she'd seen and heard, the uncertainty of whether it had all been a show for her benefit or had been real. Did she just witness a sacrifice and a massacre, or had it all happened in her mind?

Hanaawa masked his concern for her with false joviality, which quickly faded when she took up a position next to Father Time. They both crossed their arms and stared towards the bow of the vessel.

"This is the land of my birth, and I have another stop for you," Father Time announced.

Captain de Ibarra didn't like the sound of what Father Time might 'have'—as it was becoming clear that once the usefulness of his ship and crew expired, so would Tempus's reason for keeping them. He shared a look of concern with Hanaawa, who had heard the same finality in the pronouncement.

"White Apple here will tell you where to go. You will obey her as you would obey me, or face my wrath just as if you dared cross me!"

"Where White Apple leads," Hanaawa said, "we would follow, as she has earned our trust and respect." Captain de Ibarra raised his eyebrow at this, but was silent.

"Just stop," she snapped at her uncle. "I know what you're trying to do, but stop! I've made up my mind, and I make my own decisions."

"Ignore them," Father Time decreed. "Focus. Where are we going?"

Feeling for the answer within herself, White Apple was silent. It was like trying to see something that evaded being seen directly, and only became clear if she focused elsewhere. "Where you've already been," she said.

Distracting her, Father Time also insulted her. "Yes, fool. Anyone could guess that. Don't make me ask again, or you will be the one feeling my wrath!"

The sun was rising, and appeared as a bright blob on the southeast horizon. "Look to the sundog on the left," White Apple shouted as a halo of light appeared around the orb. As the sun climbed upwards, she called to Captain de Ibarra, "Take a reading on that sundog, now."

"Aye," he answered, looking at Hanaawa as he lifted his sextant. As soon as he got the bearing, twenty-two degrees to the left of the rising sun, parhelic circles and tangent arcs burst from the light of the sun before being obscured by clouds. To the rest of the crew, as the sun rose, the light faded, and Ireland resumed its gray wintry appearance. But to White Apple, lines of energy crisscrossed the land and remained when she looked for them.

"They're ancient conduits of power," White Apple said, as if the idea was something she'd lived her whole life around.

"Yes, they are, White Obvious," Father Time denigrated her, although it was far from obvious to anyone else on the *Agility*, who could neither perceive them nor could they have understood the implications had they been able to. "And if you were any help at all, you'd get this miserable crew to make haste for our destiny!" He paused, then laughed. "Ha! I meant destination!"

PART THREE: The World at War

Seramis enraged, and using hitherto undreamt of abilities.

Chapter Eleven: A Choice

In which some are reunited and some are left behind

The mood was markedly grimmer in London when Lady Seramis returned than when she had left. The storms and freezing cold that had continued through the spring and now into summer—a word that itself now held no contemporary meaning—had displaced all the usual activity, and the empty streets saw only occasional soldiers. Their drills and marching punctuated the days with martial displays before each unit was to be sent to Hanover in preparation for war. In addition to the forboding weather and the forbidding soldiers—both of which had settled everywhere in London— sadness following the loss of the king's sister darkened the atmosphere even further.

Seramis seemed to gravitate towards Henry as they rode up the Thames towards Westminster. He was quick to engage Seramis's intellect and give her the time she needed to heal from the horror she had witnessed. Compounding the pain of witnessing the execution of her friend and benefactor was the grim realization that she could still quite easily follow the path of retribution and destruction that Father Time had apparently chosen. Despite her inner pain and confusion, she felt grounded in Henry's presence. She also felt guilty about how she had rejected him, yet the present was not quite the time to make amends for a personal slight.

Long after the rest of the officers had gone to their individual commands, Lord Albion lingered with her.

"I feel like I'm keeping you," Lady Seramis said as they rode in a coach towards Blackfriars.

"You aren't... I mean, you will... I..." He laughed. "I'm not very good at expressing myself, except directly."

"And when all this is over"—she said, drawing closer to him—"I would prefer your direct expression as opposed to protocol or practiced charm."

"Oh, I can yet practice, milady." Henry looked away in hopes of hiding his shyness.

"And I can acknowledge your natural charm, milord." She placed a gloved hand upon his arm. "But now I must go, as I'm expected at the Christmas-Court-turned-Theater-of-War, and you must return to the Admiralty."

"It's just up Fleet Street, of course!" He leaned in to Lady Seramis. "I look forward to our next meeting."

"I look forward to our every meeting," she replied, and leaned upwards to kiss him on the cheek.

The Revelries of King George II had completely changed in tone, if not in energy, as the Blackfriars Theatre was given over to tables holding maps and plans for the contingency of war from the celebrations of the holidays that had replaced the now-seasonally-inappropriate High Summer Festival. As Seramis made her way past the bonfires surrounding the entrance, rumors of the revolts in the colonies were trickling into the halls of power. Of course, the full extent of the chaos and the involvement of the other powers with interests in the New World was complete guesswork. The lack of communication—brought about by the end of regular commerce ships sailing up the Gulf Stream—spoke volumes of the immensity of the problem. When Bermuda went dark last summer, it caused alarm and shock at the news. Now that the entire American continent had gone silent, the current reaction was one of grim resignation in imagining the worst.

When Lady Seramis Helleborine was announced, the king cleared the theatre, much to the surprise of the generals and admirals brought into the crisis late in its development. In spite of the officers' protestations the counselors privy to her mission and personal involvement accelerated their egress. When they were alone, both monarch and subject fell into each other's embrace and unashamedly wept.

"My Liege, I am so sorry that I did nothing to save your sister!"

Attempting to recover, the king whispered, "Did she ever tell you how close we were? When our mother was banished from England?"

Seramis could only shake her head as she wept.

"There was a clavichord—no, a harpsichord, I think—that she used to play," the king said unsteadily. "Did you ever play it?" She nodded while she sobbed, and he continued. "It had a compartment where we would hide our toys, calling it 'our treasure' and, in case anything were to happen to one of us..." At that he broke down in huge, wracking cries of grief.

"I will always personally regret not paying closer attention to our sister's warning," the king wailed. "Why did we send you into the spider's web?"

"Sire, please don't blame yourself." Seramis tried to recover, and curtseyed. "I failed both her and you when I should have worked out the plan that would have saved us all!"

King George II straightened and raised her up with his own hand. "We both failed, and we both have much to ask with regards to forgiveness." He chose his next words carefully. "But the original plan's author has also begged forgiveness, and spent each morning before breaking his fast and each night after his supper, in repentant prayer—"

"Sire, forgive my interruption, but do you mean Voltaire?" Uncontrolled indignation rose in her voice. "That cheese-eating—"

"I have asked much of you," the king interrupted. "And I will ask more of you still, but not without your acceptance as Dame Commander of our order. Our order has rules, and so does the secret society that counts both Voltaire and the pretender Frederick Wilhelm II, whom you know as Fritz."

"Your Majesty, as our purposes align in restoring justice and seeing it done, you already have my answer."

"And if our purposes cease to align?"

"Sire, I will see your will done as my last accomplishment in your service," Seramis replied. Her gaze was steady and her eyelids hooded as she looked hard at the monarch.

"I understand your meaning well," King George said.

"My liege, might I ask if you are a member of this society you mention?"

"Truly I am not," the king said. "I will let Voltaire answer more on that topic for himself." He rang a tiny bell. A counselor peeked through the opening between the doors, and with merely a nod from the king, fetched the Frenchman.

Sheepishly, Voltaire made his way to them, throwing himself at their feet. "I beg you forgive me, or pass judgment upon me as you wish, as I am entirely at your mercy."

"Was it a mercy that you provoked a mad and cruel monarch?" Seramis asked furiously. "Was it a mercy that you abandoned our king's sister without so much as passing along any of your plans?" Her voice rose in volume and shook with anger. "Was it?"

"I humbly apologize," was all Voltaire said and all he could say.

"Did you give Princess Sophie Dorothea or me the chance at sane judgment? Did begging make any difference then?" Her eyes swam with hot tears.

"I cannot give you any answers, as my society has made me swear an unbreakable oath, which my superior, Frederick Wilhelm II, repeated upon me—"

"And you think this absolves you?" Controlling the tremor in her voice, Lady Seramis maintained a cool, soft, dangerously calm tone. "Your hands are covered in blood—"

The king interrupted. "One more shall answer for his actions, Lady Seramis, or at least, provide some answers..." Once again he summoned a counselor, and after a similar exchange, the pretender to the Prussian throne—he had once been the heir apparent, the crown prince—entered. He did

The Fury of Storms

not throw himself upon the mercy of Lady Seramis, as he was as haughty and reserved as his father was insane.

"I believe the discussion centers around my late mother," the pretender said in a cultured voice. Fritz, as he was known, was handsome, tall, and in nearly all things was the leader that Prussia deserved and that his father was not. "The situation is this: the Hapsburgs and Hohenzollerns have no love for Prussia. They and the remaining states of the Holy Roman Empire align themselves against the Mad King. But now, France and mighty England have joined their united cause—inspired by you and Voltaire here—in demanding a change in the regime—"

Seramis was livid. "Was your mother a mere pawn in your geopolitical game, Fritz?" Disdain dripped from her lips.

"You don't know what you yourself have started, Marchioness," Fritz said, clutching his feathered tricorn tight. "The nations of Europe are united without having been conquered, as has never happened before."

"What does that have to do with the brutal execution of your mother?" Her anger was unapologetic.

"Her blood is on my hands, Dame Commander, but do you think her the only one who died on my behalf?" Fritz said, suddenly looking like the pained young man he was. "You would neither have seen nor heard of the execution of Hans von Katte—he who was more than a friend to me. Do you think my escape was mere happenstance? My mother did not know of it—Voltaire had no idea—but I had been planning for months to flee my father. Not for political reasons but for a love that has no name—"

"Enough," commanded the king, trembling in his attempt at self-control. "I don't think it's merely the time I've spent

179

among the English, nor that my sister fell prey to your father, but such bloody transitions belong to a past better left behind."

"Your Majesty, I will yield to my noble and wise uncle in all matters," Fritz said, struggling with heartfelt sorrow for the first time that Seramis had witnessed. "And I repeat my most sincere apologies. If I had known the outcome before I had started, I never—"

"I know, Nephew." Compassion returned to his voice. Turning, he addressed Seramis. "Will you yield in your anger, Cambridgeshire? Will you accept the current and future repentance of these men, in combination with a future of equality?"

"What do you mean, Your Majesty?" Her anger at the passing of her friend cooled into a fury born of sadness at the mounting losses.

"While the injustice visited upon Fritz and Hans is still an issue, my sister needn't have been subservient to the Mad King if she had been queen of Hanover and his equal. Salic law—the centuries-old rule that prevents a woman from wearing a crown on the continent—shall be repealed as a direct result of her martyrdom. Women shall be able to rule in the states of the empire." He approached Lady Seramis, placing his hand upon her shoulder. "It is a small step, but a positive one. Her sacrifice—and your suffering—have made it possible."

The Fury of Storms

"This is our chance, and we be fools not to take it!" Captain de Ibarra exclaimed, huddled in close with Hanaawa and the McClures. The four of them crowded on the wheel deck, despite the late hour. Father Time and White Apple had again left the *Agility* in order to scout out some mysterious power that only they could sense.

"We're taking an awful chance just discussing this," Mrs. McClure pointed out, "and you know it! He knows things that no one could possibly—"

"We may have to take greater chances," Ibarra interrupted, "and I think we've taken awful risks already." He peered out the door, looking for eavesdroppers, but saw no one. "We face annihilation every moment we're around that monster, there's no denying!"

"You're proposing abandoning a girl to Father Time's clutches," Mrs. McClure said. "If we leave now, we've washed our hands of one of our own—is that a line we're all willing to cross?"

"How do you know she's still one of us?" her husband asked. "Hanaawa, didn't you say that Father Time manipulated the slaves and natives of Virginia colony by entering their dreams? Has he found a way to change White Apple's feelings of loyalty and friendship, without even her knowing about it?"

Ibarra didn't give the war chief time to respond. "I'm so sorry, Hanaawa, but your niece may already be in Father Time's clutches, and there's naught we can do about it."

"I don't know that," Hanaawa said solemnly. "And I refuse to let her go."

"Still, don't we have a mission?" McClure asked.

"Aye, and if we're to find Dame Commander Seramis and report what we know, we have to start looking for her right away," the captain said.

The darkness shrouded the impasse among the friends, as the colonel wanted to press the matter, but a look from his wife silenced him.

"You must leave, but I will not be joining you," Hanaawa said, breaking the impasse. "You are all in danger, as all of us are in danger of being dispensed with when the mood strikes Father Time." He stepped away from the group, as if to begin the separation immediately.

"Are you..." Ibarra shouted two words, then closed his mouth and made fists with both hands as if holding fast to his temper. "Have you gone mad?" The question came out as a whisper.

"But how can you do this?" Mrs. McClure asked. "White Apple has had some small influence over Father Time since the beginning. But what can you possibly do to protect yourself?... And didn't you say that he threatened you in a dream?"

"White Apple is not only my niece, she will also be the matriarch of my clan, and I have been bound to her fate," Hanaawa declared as he backed away. "I'm sorry, but you've seen that she may even become a powerful danger to you all just as much as Father Time is. It's for her sake that I urge you now to leave. White Apple may lose all that she is unless she retains a connection to her past—a connection to how it was before everything changed."

All four shared the same, determined look, as if fear and sorrow had been driven out of them and left only anger and resolve in their wake. It lasted but a moment, until Mrs.

McClure rushed forth to hug Hanaawa at the same time Captain de Ibarra lunged to do the same, nearly colliding with her only to stop just in time. After saying farewell, Hanaawa collected his things while the crew prepared to launch. Swinging over the side on a guy rope, the chief waited until the *Agility* floated low over solid land to drop to the frozen ground. The airship became smaller, ever smaller, as it floated high away to the southeast.

Chapter Twelve: A Re-union

In which plans are made and mysteries revealed

Captain de Ibarra had considered the wisdom of flying the airship directly into London and found it wanting, to say the least. Cloud cover had made floating over England's midlands an uneventful journey, but now that they were on the water, the situation changed. Just sailing up the Thames, *The Agility of Clouds* had been challenged a half-dozen times by ice-covered ships on the nearly frozen river. A gentle snow had been falling steadily and the captain had taken to keeping the ship's papers on hand, as boarder after boarder inspected the craft and went away puzzled.

Hints of Lady Seramis's reputation had apparently made their way through the Royal Navy, and many wondered at the strange contraptions on the vessel but received only silence for their questions after an invitation to take up the matter with the admiralty. Had Ibarra known that the owner of his vessel was at that very moment in conference with the king, he would have undoubtedly mentioned that, as well.

But such mention was not warranted, as long as the *Agility* sailed under the King's colors, had no armament to speak of, and kept its paperwork in order. After all, more pressing concerns were at hand as England prepared for war. The police state that was the English government before the Reformation had lessened with more liberal policies and their economic drivers, but the martial attitude infected everyone who boarded the *Agility*. Personal hostility was the order of the day, and Ibarra bit his tongue on several occasions.

"Mission or no mission, I'm not going to make it to London without exploding—this I warn, Colonel!" he called out.

"You've gotten us this far!" Colonel McClure replied.

"Well, you may have to get us the rest of the way."

"Not me! I have no desire to take over this vessel!"

"Then ask the missus if she would be so kind as take lessons in sailing," the captain said. "Because it may just come to that!"

Barges under heavy escort were emptying London of soldiers and supplies. At times, the *Agility* was forced to wait until dozens of craft passed it by through an ice-choked channel. The benefit from the constant traffic was that there were still navigable channels cleared of ice along the Thames. Unfortunately for a city that thrived on trade, few merchant vessels were making the journey this far inland, except for the half-dozen that had been turned back from heading further north.

"Do you truly think London will be the best place to start looking for Lady Seramis?" asked Captain de Ibarra. The bosun manned the wheel, but the captain kept a close eye on the river and the ice while talking to Colonel McClure. "Isn't her home in Cambridge-something?" he asked.

"If we can't get word to her, then we could try that Albion fellow in the Admiralty," the colonel answered. "But we won't have papers to go beyond the docks at Wapping where we were instructed to berth."

"Oh, I can get papers, if we need 'em." Ibarra's eyes glinted.

"Let's hope that won't be necessary," Mrs. McClure said. She had joined them on the quarterdeck, wrapped in a cloth overcoat.

"I mean to find out what we can before movin' on," Ibarra explained, "but as spies go, I might not exactly blend in." He laughed. "And your large husband here definitely stands out. It might just be you, missus, who gets to reconnoiter! Do you have time for lessons in espionage as well as sailing?"

"Enjoy your little joke, Captain!" Mrs. McClure said, wrapping herself even tighter against the cold.

"I do, but I hide the honest truth wrapped up in jollity. I hate to think we abandoned Hanaawa and White Apple for nothing!"

The Fury of Storms

"We've yet to hear any word, have we?" Colonel McClure asked the assembled crew. They had been at the Wapping docks since morning, and although the light of day hadn't changed, it was now noon. The snow had stopped, but it was still bitter cold and cloudy. The docks were crowded with empty vessels that had no destination now that trade had effectively ceased with the colonies. On the same pier as the *Agility*, tall triple-masted merchant ships crowded next to the airship, which looked like nothing more than an old fashioned caravel.

While there was some traffic along the docks despite the lack of commercial activity, it was light until a squad of the king's cavalry cantered up to the airship, a single coach coming along after. The cavalry formed a detail as the coach drew near the airship. The crew lined up along the port rails while the captain and the McClures stood on the aft quarterdeck. All were arrayed to welcome the expected owner, Lady Seramis. A footman opened the door, revealing a seated figure wearing a resplendent gown in the shadows within the coach.

But after a moment, Ibarra frowned. "Well?"

Colonel McClure was likewise puzzled. "What is she waiting for?"

"Time waits for no one!" The voice, a clear contralto, came from behind the assembled group. Turning as if struck, the captain and the McClures were wide-eyed at the sudden intrusion and the unexpected voice.

"Forgive me, please, good friends!" Seramis exclaimed and rushed forward from the wheelhouse, where she had silently dropped to the deck from ratlines on the mizzenmast.

Covering her captured hand in kisses, Captain de Ibarra admonished, "What in heaven's secret name did you think you were doing?" Both the McClures had simultaneously embraced her and exclaimed their delight so loudly that it immediately attracted the attention of the rest of the crew.

"Oh, good friends, to see you when I feared the worst warms my heart in this chill!" Seramis proclaimed. "When I got word that you were here, I knew two things immediately, and I dreaded what they would portend: one, you had succeeded in finding Father Time; and two, disaster had befallen the colonies."

"Right on both counts," Colonel McClure said. "And I see that you have been busy yourself. But what is this?" he asked, gently holding her arms as he appraised her. "Is this a new fashion in London?"

Seramis was wearing the same form-fitting leather garments she had worn when she had sneaked into Paris. "They are a bit more continental, I think," she said. "I had to leave someone as bait in the coach, in case Father Time had followed or trapped you!" Lady Seramis explained. "You might recall the last time I met with him, he dispensed with all pretense..."

"Of course," the colonel continued. "You're nearly right on all counts. Father Time had indeed captured us all but we escaped and we have much to tell you." Smiling, he shook his head as he continued to appraise her. "As functional as your attire appears, I don't know if I'll get used to seeing you like this!"

"I don't mind the attire—it's the drama!" the captain explained, laughing. "How did you manage that? You must have climbed the rigging of... Oh, never you mind me! I

The Fury of Storms

should expect the unexpected. But after that entrance, Mrs. McClure will likely refuse any and all lessons in espionage now..."

Laughing, Mrs. McClure said, "Actually, now that I see it involves more comfortable clothing, I may take it up. Could you get used to seeing me dressed in this?" She tilted her head toward her husband, her eyes sparkling.

Unable as he was to answer, Colonel McClure's eyes grew wide at the suggestion and his mouth opened and closed silently.

Wishing to focus their energies, Seramis gestured to their baggage and glanced at each in turn, frowning slightly. "Friends, gather your things, we have accommodations for you and the crew, and much to discuss. But first, where are Hanaawa and White Apple?"

"Wretches!" Father Time screamed. Words from the Bard came to him:

"They Shall to my flaming wrath be oil and flax.
Henceforth I will not have to do with pity!"

While Father Time raged about the unseasonably cold rural landscape, White Apple ignored him. Instead, she sensed and followed the direction of the wind, letting her senses feel how the gusts had blown up and to the east. She cast her senses out further, and the gusts, highlighted with a silver light only she could see, started to roll backwards. She followed them until they were disturbed by a large shape where the lake was clear of ice. Turbulence along the surface of the frozen lake was cast in the wake of a leeward disturbance, the shape of which was beginning to take form in White Apple's eyes. It was the *Agility*, or rather the wind the airship had displaced many hours ago, which White Apple could perceive as if its outlines were still visible.

Through tracing the currents of air that once wafted around the craft, she watched the ghostly outline of the airship cast off and ascend, until a figure appeared to drop to the ground and make for the tree line on the shore. All this made perfect sense to White Apple, in that if one could roll back the effects, one could understand the causes. But she had never been able to so easily visualize so much from so little evidence. Never before had the wind yielded its secrets as she had just witnessed.

"Wretches! Miserable pus-filled scum!" Father Time screamed, ignorant of his apprentice's newfound ability. "Faithless failures!" He ranted at the invisible crew of the *Agility* who had stranded him and White Apple in Ireland. "I should have cut off half your limbs and sewn pairs of you traitors together. Oh, but that is nothing compared to what I shall do now!" He threatened the air with hideous tortures and empty promises of vengeance. "My mercy will never again manifest itself!" He shouted at the sky and the trees, all of which continued their existence heedless of his fury.

As did someone or something in the trees that was hiding there, White Apple realized. It had scarcely left a trail, hardly a footprint in the snow, and it was absolutely and incredibly still, whatever it was. But it was watching, and waiting, and also ignoring Father Time's rant.

"...And what good are you, anyway?" Father Time turned his rage upon White Apple.

"Shall I go fetch the airship while you stay here?" White Apple asked, evenly and without emotion. "Or shall I start the construction of another vessel for you?"

Father Time considered his apprentice and her offer of assistance. She was too intelligent to be simply ordered about. But what was her motivation? "You're just a girl, and hardly even a worthy test of my powers." Father Time extended his senses to perceive her thoughts, to fold her feelings into a malleable collection of fears and desires, focused entirely upon himself.

White Apple stood up straight, feeling his invasive attentions as a pressure upon her temples and a chill up and down her spine. She didn't attempt to resist, but she didn't need to. His intrusion was halted.

With a roar he sprang at her, who didn't flinch at his attack. He glared at the child as he stood mere inches away from his target. Visualizing points of weakness and finding none, Father Time lifted his hand to strike the girl when the sky cracked, and all light was torn away from horizon to horizon.

When Father Time lifted his hand to her, Hanaawa dropped from the tree onto the snowy ground beneath. In the moment between his leaving the tree and reaching the ground, the sky opened with a loud crack. Instantly everywhere was black. His eyes couldn't adjust, as there was no light, but he had the scene before him in his mind's eye, and Hanaawa didn't hesitate as he ran blindly but unerringly towards his niece.

Of course, it would be Uncle, thought White Apple as she stood on the frozen lake where the *Agility* had left hours ago. She recognized the sound of his running as he headed straight for her. She, too, could see no visible light, but was still looking towards where Father Time was standing. He had frozen in nearly the same pose, ready to strike at her.

She could still sense the wind buffeting about him, as revealed in faint tracings of perceived turbulence, lines of forces both physical and metaphysical swirling about him. And now, with the distraction of visible light removed—How? she wondered—she could see Father Time even as he could not see himself. Faint temporal shadows, like hollow dolls that followed Father Time where he had been, guided her. His tantrum was still present, as if frozen in pantomime, and each shaken fist and stomped foot had been recorded as it left a mark in time that White Apple now knew how to look for.

It was an amazing sight, but not nearly as fascinating as what she was just about to discover. Her uncle's arrival delayed that discovery, permitting her but a glimpse before she heard him draw nearer.

White Apple stepped back to avoid her uncle's heroic attempt to snatch her from danger. She had surmised that he, too, could not see anything, and was acting upon memory, which he had been. But like her, he was listening carefully, and he heard her step back—and he assumed it was because either she didn't know who was rushing to save her, or she was backing away from Father Time. It simply didn't occur to Hanaawa that White Apple didn't want to be saved.

He adjusted his trajectory upon hearing her movements, and was upon her before she could step farther. Picking her up, he carried her at a run towards the still invisible far shore, ignoring the gentle but persistent tapping on the back of his head: her, trying to get his attention, but not wanting to draw Father Time's attention to herself with Hanaawa vulnerable. She continued tapping even as he stopped, now out of Father Time's earshot.

"What? Why are you doing that?" Hanaawa whispered.

"I wanted to get your attention," White Apple said matter-of-factly. She went on in the same emotionless tone. "I also wanted you to feel a mere fraction of the pressure that Father Time will be able to inflict upon your skull without even lifting a finger."

"My thanks for the warning!" Hanaawa said. "Why did you want my attention?"

"Just two little things: go away." She looked hard at his pained expression.

Hanaawa set White Apple down, a bit nonplussed at the emphasis in her delivery, if not the message itself.

"But why?" Hanaawa looked hurt.

White Apple didn't care.

"You're in danger here, obviously!" she hissed, shaking her head. "Why do you have to be this way? I don't want you here. I don't need you!"

"Well, here I am. And so are..." His voice trailed off as he looked over her head to where Father Time was staring as well, at the only two things visible in this part of the world: two things that Hanaawa could neither identify nor comprehend.

"Who?" She turned around as well. Her eyes grew wider in terror or perhaps in awe, also completely unable to apprehend what they were seeing.

Chapter Thirteen: A Goal

In which new skills are learned

The crew of the *Agility* slept in actual beds, ate fresh food, and rested while Lady Seramis learned about the destruction wrought by Father Time in the colonies, worried about the absence of Hanaawa and White Apple, and debated about what to do next.

"It seems clear that we need to extricate White Apple and Hanaawa from Patrick Tempus's—Father Time's—clutches," Seramis pointed out.

"I'm not so sure White Apple is extricate-able, milady," Captain de Ibarra noted. In front of him were untouched dishes and trays from his dinner. Apparently, he could only nervously pick at them, yet he was not alone in having lost his appetite to the concern he felt for departed friends. Leaning back, he spoke with regret. "Even Hanaawa wasn't sure anymore, but he did stay with her out of devotion."

"Don't fault yourself for leaving," Mrs. McClure said. "We all agreed upon the decision. Judging by what is going on here, we've got to look at the bigger picture!"

"What do you mean?" Seramis asked. She had exchanged her usual garb for a dress similar to what Mrs. McClure wore, without Sarah's accessories of belt and holstered flintlock pistol. Sarah was well-practiced in the use of firearms, whereas Seramis was not. For her part, Seramis wore the medallion of her order, out of respect for its traditions and with a militaristic bearing she felt matched her mood.

"Father Time thrives on chaos—or, it is somehow his mission to sow discord and dispute wherever he goes," Mrs. McClure said.

"I can only imagine what life was like in Virginia Colony before you left." Seramis shook her head in sorrow. "I hope that it will improve now that Father Time has left and returned to the place of his birth."

"If Hanaawa were here, he'd be able to tell you firsthand some of Father Time's techniques," Colonel McClure said. He didn't approve of Hanaawa's staying in Ireland, but he admired his friend's courage and conviction, nonetheless. "Judging by what happened in the colonies, an extended war in Europe will only play right into Father Time's hands. Both sides in Virginia Colony seemed to be manipulated—their anger was baited and twisted until they weren't even rational. We have to take care that we don't fall into the same trap."

"I think my husband is right," Mrs. McClure said. "But we've all felt the effects of Father Time's presence in our dreams. If only Hanaawa had the skill to somehow identify and—further—do battle with him on that level."

Ibarra nodded. "Tactically, we absolutely need to engage Father Time on his level, or somehow gain the advantage so we can surprise him. While I don't think he'll be expecting us to return for our friends, unless we have some way to even the odds, there's no way we can capture him like we did before."

Colonel McClure stroked his chin thoughtfully. "If we try now to assist Hanaawa and somehow help White Apple, I'm afraid that we will fail, and miss the opportunity to do some good where it will be needed. Lady Seramis, will you go to war to prevent it from becoming more widespread?"

"Truthfully, that's one of the few contradictions that I haven't been able to resolve! And yes, Colonel, I think I see your point." Lady Seramis stood and walked around the table so she could face them all. "It is clear that there will soon be war in Europe, and while it appears that Prussia is outnumbered and has been outmaneuvered diplomatically, its army can outgun and outfight any other that can be fielded..."

"But didn't you say that nearly all the rest of Europe is allied against Prussia? How can it stand against that combination?" Strategy was at the front of the colonel's thoughts.

"Sadly, only England is marching to puts its forces in harm's way, although the king's forces in Hanover may also be counted upon," she said. "If Prussia knew this, it wouldn't hesitate to move on Hanover. But that hesitation has given England time to take up its position."

She put her hands on the table. "While the rest of Europe—joining in the dream of unification that is the League of Augsburg—agrees in principle on eradicating a mad monarch from power, each state only sees its own interest in the matter and feels that it will serve its interests better by being averse to risk." Sighing, she continued. "It is enough, however, that France and the states of the Holy Roman Empire agree to allow England to maneuver in Europe—that was almost too much to hope for in itself. Of course, for Spain and Portugal to agree not to take advantage of this opportunity may yet prove to be decisive. England can concentrate on the job at hand—although I have been assured that its navy is on reserve if Spain changes its mind."

"That's exactly the point," McClure said. "If the alliance falls, and the Spanish Armada becomes ascendant once again, then Father Time will only need to provide the spark to ignite all that dry powder. The devastation of the Thirty Years' War will be nothing in comparison. If there had been formal armies and not just militia in the colonies, the fighting would have gone on and on to the last soldier standing..."

Captain de Ibarra stood and straightened his leather coat as if attending a formal function. "If you want to go to the aid of White Apple I will follow, but under protest!"

"Sir!" Seramis said, surprised. "Please speak your piece, as I would rather hear your adjuration now than bear your admonition later!"

"We can perhaps hasten an end to this war. I know you've never held with my wishes to arm the *Agility*, but a floating man-o-war could prove decisive. No army, no matter how experienced, will have any chance at resisting an unopposed force from above."

"Is that what we've become, good captain?" she asked. "Are we reduced to choosing between more efficient means of destruction and less certain chances of survival while effecting a rescue?"

Colonel McClure also stood. "Milady, if we could effect a rescue, what then? Will we be able to stop Father Time? We must do both if we go to White Apple's aid, and then hope that good fortune favors England's armies. Otherwise, we could fail and lose all."

"Gentlemen," Mrs. McClure said. "Please sit, as we don't even know if Father Time and White Apple are still in

Ireland." She touched her husband's arm gently. "There's no reason at all to think that they won't leave once they've concluded their business. If Father Time follows the same pattern, he's already on the continent stirring what trouble he can."

Seramis sighed. "I, too, should follow your wise counsel, madam, as I started the provocation. But also"—she paused for a moment while she sat down—"I am convinced.

"Let us to war," she said quietly. "Yet again."

Two beings, made of gold, each with the light of the sun shining from glowing globes above their featureless faces, stood where Father Time had been staring. He had been transfixed by their appearance, even before they materialized. He had seen time itself shift as a processional to their arrival. Now it seemed that all light was gone from the world except that which came from these two.

"The gods!" Hanaawa whispered reverently, as he, too, stared at the new arrivals. They were at least twenty feet tall, stood an equal distance apart, and were identical and—to Hanaawa—impressive in every way. He was awestruck. "They shine with the light of the sun!"

White Apple was not as impressed. "Those lights are just lanterns!" she whispered dismissively. "Neither of them are the Sun King of our legends. Look! They glow with polished metal. See? Those are not jewels radiant with power, but crystals lit from within." Her gift of sight was at this moment a practical one, and she pushed him behind a tree now visible due to the 'lanterns' as she had described. "Their helms are faced with a polished glass, like mirrors, but they could see us from within them, unless we hide!"

"What use is hiding from a god?" Hanaawa rightfully asked.

"What use is there arguing with me? Either get down or get out of the way!" She joined him as he heeded her and slipped behind a tree.

"You do not think these mere men, do you?"

"If I have to repeat your own teachings to you, I'll push you out in front of them myself! But since you've lost your judgment, I'll remind you: what you would call a god is just a being with differing abilities!"

"I see. So, let's not attract those different abilities, then, eh?"

"Uggh!" White Apple groaned, then sighed with exasperation before peeking around the tree trunk. She stiffened at the sight.

"What is it?" He made a move to look, but she pushed him down. He didn't resist, so her diminutive frame was able to push him bodily against the tree.

"Father Time is being pulled apart—even as I watch," White Apple exclaimed in hushed tones. "He doesn't bleed, however. Like when his throat was slit—"

"What?" Hanaawa exclaimed. "When did you—?"

"Shhh!" White Apple said. "His limbs have been separated from his body by the two beings—apparently using light to pull on them and hold his body in place." She sounded disinterested but curious. "It appears to be quite painful."

"Could these be newfound allies?" Hanaawa asked.

"I don't think so," White Apple said. "Father Time appeared to know them and was both defiant and supplicating when they appeared." She shook her head. "But I wouldn't care for the results he's getting." She turned away in disgust. "It is truly painful to even watch, although it couldn't have happened to a more deserving—"

"What do you mean? Have you really joined in league with him?"

"What if I have? It's my choice—my choice, Uncle! And what I've chosen is to learn!" She looked at him and shook her head. "And, oh, what I have learned!" Smiling despite the torture taking place just out of sight, she laughed, exuberant. "I have spent an entire life seeing just the tiniest fraction of existence, and understanding only a little more than that! Now I see almost everything. It is amazing—astounding—what I can now see—"

"But have you understood any more?"

"What? Why would you ask such a thing?" White Apple became sullen and despondent. "How could you say that?"

"You know how proud I am of you, how much I respect your accomplishments and your abilities, White Apple, but this is beyond what anyone could hope to understand..."

"I understand. I do—or if I don't, I wi—" A terrifying shriek exploded from Father Time, a sound of desperate agony and unimaginable pain.

"He's holding out much longer than I thought," she commented dispassionately. "But this is when they'll really start—well, they already have. But that will all be mere preamble to what they have in store for him." Slowly she peeked around the trunk of the tree.

The torture of Father Time was brutal and unrelenting, and he could have perished at several points at the hands of his tormentors—his immaterial form stripped of coherence in the most painful way imaginable—but for a last-moment change of mind either to prolong the agony or to offer a possible reprieve from an ultimate and final judgment.

Father Time had been warned that he faced such punishment for any delays, but he could neither respond in his defense nor plead for mercy as the pain prevented even the most basic thought or response. In his prior life as a spy, Patrick was not unused to torture, as either inflictor or recipient, but it had never, ever been like this. He had never before yearned so desperately and wordlessly for the sweet release of death, and when it nearly came upon him, and he almost succumbed to merciful oblivion but failed to slip into the unconsciousness of that final slumber, the realization that he yet lived sent him into utter despondence.

Broken and whimpering when the torture finally finished, Father Time only wanted to do anything and everything ever asked of him by his masters. The pain still lasted, its intensity only slowly fading, but where before had existed confusion and silent misery, he now felt a love and gratitude toward his torturers for ending the anguish he had felt. Lying prostrate before the invaders, he sobbed in supplication, murmuring phrases of devotion in his suffering. So devout was he that he almost missed his new instructions, as spoken by one of his masters.

"Your objective is to break apart the new union of this planet's most powerful organizations," the invader on Father Time's right began. "The militarized governments to the south and east of this island, in the place you call Europe, are about to take their first steps toward union, and you must stop it. There will be a battle, or series of battles if you are successful in prolonging the action, starting at Lauenburg on the Elbe River in Saxe-Lauenburg between those whom you call the Prussians and the English..."

Crying out and interrupting, Father Time begged, "Please let me destroy the English for you!" He got to his knees as he pleaded.

"No, not entirely," said the other to his left. "We must involve all of the armed forces before they can be destroyed. You will find you have allies that converge upon that position for you to control."

"Just as we control you," said the first to have spoken. "We are very disappointed that you have delayed here, as you could have set many traps and stirred up resentment instead of pursuing your own aims."

"Yes! Yes, I did what you asked there in the New World!" Father Time said, slowly getting to his feet. "Was it not exactly to your liking? All I need is more time and I can do the same in Europe!"

"There is no more time. The final confrontation is almost upon us. Why didn't you proceed directly to Europe as we commanded?" the second asked.

White Apple, listening from her hiding place, wondered at their ignorance, as they surely could have traced the time streams as she was able to do and recreated the events that had transpired. She herself wondered at the echoes that she and Hanaawa—and even Father Time—left, but quickly realized that the two beings left no traces. Is it possible that they are somehow outside of time itself?

"Uncle!" White Apple whispered, "I think even Father Time is but a pawn..." but she never finished, as Tempus had just answered the others.

"I have been training an apprentice!" he exclaimed in partial answer to the question. Despite the love he would now profess for his masters, and despite the cruel punishments he had just received, he dared to lie about his ambitions and omit from his answer the elements of his coveting the airship and desiring vengeance against Lady Seramis.

"Another?" asked the two beings in unison, moving forward in an unspoken threat. Father Time cried out and dropped to his knees Their shouts shook the air. "Where?"

Hanaawa wished that he and White Apple hadn't lingered but would have gone as quickly as possible after they had left Father Time's side. His wish was especially poignant now that all the trees and any other possible cover had vanished. Both masters and servant all turned their faces towards the now exposed Hanaawa and White Apple in concert. Hanaawa stood upright and stepped in front of her as he began to walk towards them.

"All your accomplishments—every deed—all will be forgotten, Father Time!" Hanaawa shouted as he walked, gaining their attention and trying to buy time for White Apple to escape. "In fact, your very name will die upon your lips the last time it is uttered, and no one ever will know it or anything about you!"

"This?" asked one of the others. "This is your apprentice? He doesn't sound like an apprentice..."

"But," Hanaawa continued, listening for the sound of her running, but hearing nothing—he dared not look back and give away her existence if she had not yet been noticed. "They will also forget your defeat at the hands of the Helleborine girl."

Father Time screamed, an incoherent shriek of anger. "No! This is not the one."

"There is another?" One of the beings spoke emotionlessly. "I think this one looks vaguely familiar—"

"Over there! Behind the interloper!" Tempus shouted as he pointed at White Apple, who had been standing and listening the entire time.

Hanaawa turned and whispered, concern distorting his face. "Why didn't you run?"

She answered in a voice of ice. "Why didn't you?"

"I'm trying to save you!"

"I don't want to be saved!" The final word bore all her scorn.

The Fury of Storms

"This is an emergent development," one invader said to the other.

"Most interesting," the second agreed. "It is possible that our plans will be accelerated; we must recalculate our timelines..." and they both disappeared.

Light returned to the world for the three left behind, but not for the trees, apparently, for they remained gone. Father Time was still standing upon the frozen lake where the *Agility* had last touched the surface, but Hanaawa was staring and shaking his head at White Apple.

"What?" Her indignation crackled in the cold air.

Words from the invaders lingered upon the air and echoed in the ears of those remaining. "...Break apart the new union of this planet's most powerful organizations" and "...starting at Lauenburg..." made their instructions clear.

Father Time paused to listen for only a moment before turning on Hanaawa in a rage. "What are you doing here?"

"I said it before," Hanaawa answered nonchalantly. "No one will know or ever hear about Father Time..."

"And you are now a chronicler?" Tempus asked incredulously. "Albeit a dead one?"

"He's here," White Apple said, "to try to save me!"

Hanaawa merely shook his head, only barely restraining himself from throwing his arms up in the air in exasperation.

"Well, then, since he is neither friend nor foe," Father Time said maliciously, "but merely a disinterested party, I will not break him to my will entirely nor kill him right away, but perhaps just a little of both..." With a cruel smile on his face, he started towards the war chief.

But White Apple was there first, and shoved her uncle as high as she could reach on his shoulder. With a yell, Father Time lunged at that exact moment, but missed by mere fractions of an inch. White Apple deftly stepped around Father Time, and tugged on Hanaawa's other arm, just as Father Time spun and sliced at his throat with a knife that materialized in Father Time's hand. "What is this?" the attacker cried out. "How are you doing this?"

"Oh, it's nothing," White Apple replied as once again she stepped behind Hanaawa, who was completely taken aback by the attacks and her manipulations that defeated them and apparently saved his life. White Apple pushed at the back of Hanaawa's knees, bringing him down in the instant that Father Time switched the blade from one hand to the other and stabbed at where Hanaawa's eye had been. Father Time snatched back his hand, and White Apple was there to link her arm in his before he could recover.

"How are you doing this?" Father Time yelled as White Apple pulled on his arm, like a child pulling at an adult to go a particular direction.

"Well, I can see what you're going to do before you do it." White Apple said with a natural nonchalance. The shock of hearing so distracted Father Time, he let himself be pulled away from Hanaawa.

"What?" Father Time exploded when his shock wore off.

"I can see future echoes of you," she explained. "And of my uncle, too, but not those invaders. I think they're outside of time." Blinking, she considered the answer she just gave and wondered how it could be.

Father Time's eyes narrowed and he willed himself to become larger, too big and now too immaterial—almost a vapor—to be pulled by her, and she let go. The effect upon him was that his voice slowed as he had shifted to a different time scale. "Hhhooowww doooo yyoouu knnnnooooowww?"

"Oh, we can't talk like this..." White Apple said, and to Hanaawa's astonishment, she grew taller in relation to Father Time, who was now nearing twenty feet himself. "Now we'll still be able to understand one another."

Hanaawa cried out his fear and amazement at what White Apple was doing; despite her now being twice as tall as he was, he still felt protective of her. He called for her to stop, to return to her normal size, but to her and Father Time he sounded like the buzzing of an annoying insect. She actually began to laugh.

"Do you think this is funny?" Tempus shouted at her. Sharing the same timescale as he, she heard the words as they were intended.

"No, I think this is amazing!" White Apple exclaimed, and the words rushed forth as if from a bottle that had been uncorked. "You see, it started when I could see the time trails of cause and effect..." she said, bubbling with excitement, but then corrected herself. "Actually, it started when you commanded me to see the lines of psychic energy..." she paused, thinking for a moment.

"So does that mean that you made me into this?" Shaking her head, she continued by answering her own question, "No, I don't think you could do that!" This would have normally provoked a reaction from Father Time, but he simply stared open-mouthed. "But you may have been the catalyst! Then— as I said—I could see the future choices of yours, including all possible choices where determinism hasn't been fore-ordained." She was ecstatic at the changes. "I find it extremely interesting that no matter what choices you make at certain points, where your future path forks and breaks, there are some points in your future that are actually common to all of the choices—where destiny has you by the..."

"Very well," Father Time said. "I know how that works, as I was here before you." Petulant at White Apple's swift ascendancy, he chided her. "If you've got it all worked out, what are we going to do next?"

"Well, this is the only way to travel, wouldn't you agree? We just keep growing bigger and bigger until we can simply step from here to our destination!" White Apple smiled at the thought of herself standing astride the lands that had sent the colonists, settlers, and soldiers to her home.

"What are you going to do about him?" Father Time asked, indicating her uncle. Hanaawa not only sounded like an annoying insect, but his movements now looked that way to White Apple, too. She managed to suppress her laughter as she considered the options.

"He heard the same instructions, so he'll follow us anyway. He might as well come with us..."

The Fury of Storms

"What? How?" Father Time was beside himself at the presumption of this girl whom he could have crushed on so many occasions; he was no longer sure of his ability in that regard.

"Oh? You can't do this?" White Apple said as she halted her uncle with a touch. She then gently folded space around him just so, and time around him like the folding of a cover of a pouch as well, and picked him up carefully as she grew and grew. And as she grew, she faded into immaterial existence as did Father Time, following her into the slower time scale. In contrast to the scowl he wore on his face, her visage bore a smile like none other.

Chapter Fourteen: A War

In which battle is joined for the fate of Europe

The pretender to the Prussian throne, Frederick Wilhelm II or 'Fritz' as he was called, was in nominal command of the Alliance forces as they landed in Hamburg. The English forces had their own command structure, with King George II joining his troops in returning to Hanover to avenge his sister's death, and his chief admiral, Henry Albion, Duke of Gloucester, in command of the actual landing. Fritz's former mentor, General von Schwerin, was in command of the Prussian forces, but they had been slow to move, held back either by caution or by the heavy winter. They, too, hosted their monarch, the Mad King, Frederick Wilhelm, Fritz's father. However, the Prussian forces only followed the general's orders, ignoring their king who had ordered them, for instance, to march standing on each other's shoulders so as to thus appear taller and demoralize the enemy.

The Elbe was clear of ice at present, despite the heavy chill, so Albion was instructed to take the battle barges carrying the infantry and artillery upriver as far as was navigable, while the cavalry disembarked in Hamburg so as to be ready and maneuverable. While the English dragoons were sent ahead to scout, the heavy cavalry followed more slowly. And both were replaced on the barges by experienced Hanoverian regiments that now joined the English infantry. Once the battle was joined, Albion would leave the barges to command a special signal corps, as he was a naval officer and not in command of the Hanoverian or English ground troops. The signal corps included former spies such as Voltaire, but also new optical equipment for an as-yet untested purpose. All orders would go through the signal corps, and could even be modified based on information that the original commanders may not have had when the orders were issued.

Not all of the Alliance command was as progressive as Albion, and Fritz was as cautious as his Prussian counterpart—they had shared the same training, of course—but George II was fervent in his demands for moving swiftly. When word came that the Prussian host was camped just outside of Lauenburg, Albion anticipated his king and signaled the cavalry to secure the medieval town in preparation for landing the troops there, as far forward as possible. Fritz, however, wanted to land the foot soldiers well away from the town—using it as a shield in case the enemy attacked—and assemble the troops into formations before entering Lauenburg. As a compromise, Fritz was given direct command of five regiments of Hussars.

The Prussians had not expected their opposition to get this far south so quickly. Their own scouts had been killed or captured by the dragoons of the English, so they had no word beyond the expected landfall of the English at Hamburg. Their camp was peaceful on the still wintry morning of the thirteenth of August, so peaceful they had dispensed even with posting sentries at their stations. With fifteen thousand English and Hanoverian infantry and an immense number of artillery at his back, Fritz attacked the main Prussian force of forty thousand soldiers encamped just south of Lauenburg with his entire complement, despite being outnumbered more than twenty to one.

It was this rout that Lady Seramis witnessed as the *Agility* dropped below the cloud ceiling and entered the fray. Wave after wave of Hussar riders emptied their carbine muskets at point blank range into the disoriented Prussians, woken by the shouts of the attackers and the cries of their dying comrades. The light cavalry continued straight through the center of the Prussian camp, slashing with their sabers at anything that moved and leaving a trail of destruction in their wake. Fritz himself was at the head of the column and making straight for the commanders' tents on the southern side of the camp, but the defenders had time to set up an infantry square around their leaders, barely fifty feet on a side. Fritz brought his column to a halt and reassembled his Hussars to charge the Prussian defenses.

"Why does he linger?" Colonel McClure wondered aloud as he looked through his glass. "He should get out of there if he can't sustain his charge! Do something," he shouted to the air, "don't just stand there!"

Dame Commander Seramis was also using an eyeglass, but she was searching for the Prussian heavy cavalry. "I found them!" she exclaimed. "Signal the commanders that the Prussians are about to charge their own camp!" Albion was already prepared and watching for her signal, and had his own teams ready to send messengers when needed.

"That will be the end of the Hussars if they attack, and perhaps the end as well of more than half of the Prussian infantry regiments!" the colonel said. "I guess we made our choice and have to take the bad along with the good."

"Or not! Add to the signal that we're engaging the enemy!" Seramis shouted. "Prepare for battle! Stations ready and report! Captain, take us down to the east of the Prussian camp, directly in front of the charging cavalry and stop them in their tracks!"

"Aye!" Ibarra brought the wheel about, changing the attitude of the aerial rudder. "But that's one order I never thought I'd hear! Prepare forward guns! Fire when in range!" The fire control officers started shouting their orders as the *Agility* floated down towards the battle. The airship had gone unnoticed in the heat of battle until now, for while a floating *caravel redonda* might normally attract some interest the battle to this point had focused the attentions of the combatants away from the gray skies.

When the airship unloaded cannon shot directly into the charging ranks of Prussian cavalry, however, it quite obviously attracted everyone's notice. The huge English flag of St. George flying from the vessel's stern seemed to inspire the Alliance troops while also evidently mocking the Prussian forces, as the craft appeared untouchable as it floated into battle and then soared away unscathed.

As if to add further insult to injury, while the *Agility* rose high and passed over the heads of the Prussian cavalry charge it had stopped single-handedly by pounding the leading chargers into dust, Captain de Ibarra ordered explosive ordnance dropped into the trailing ranks of the enemy. When Fritz saw that he had just narrowly avoided being overrun by the Prussian heavy cavalry—who were now attempting to regroup after taking a drubbing from cannon shot and explosives—he pulled out of the camp westward to regroup his own lines on the other side of the river.

Unfortunately for Fritz, the Höhenwald on that side of the Elbe held a surprise that neither side's forces had counted upon.

The massive forest that was the Höhenwald and circled to the south and the west of Lauenberg was an ancient and dark wood. For centuries, it had been a home to thieves, highway robbers, and other castaways. But in the last few months, driven by unseen forces they couldn't comprehend, the entirety of Europe's wanderers—the vagabonds, the dispossessed and outsiders—had converged upon the woods and made them their home. Self-sustaining to an astonishing degree due to their usual state of deprivation, a population of one hundred thousand had camped in the Höhenwald while the nation-states of Europe had absolutely no idea what was happening or why.

Because the leaders of Europe had chosen mainly to ignore the uncounted and neglected populations while the ragged were dispersed throughout the continent, they were now forced to contend with their number as the horde swarmed out of the forest. Fritz was unable to regroup, overrun by their number and their unstoppable momentum.

The Fury of Storms

Heedless of casualty, men and women of all ages—even the aged and children—rushed screaming into the Hussars. Cutting with knives, ripping with their bare hands, even tearing with their teeth, the horde fell upon the Hussars until thousands of horses and their riders lay dead or wounded. Only Fritz and a handful of officers rallied and escaped, and still more of the rabble poured out of the wood and onto the river plain.

"Where did they come from?" Seramis said as she desperately steered the airship towards the new battle.

White Apple appeared on the main deck of the *Agility,* materializing in the midst of the crew, looking for all her powers just like any dark-skinned maiden of colonial Virginia. "Hello! Permission to come aboard?"

"Where did you come from?" the captain said, echoing the Dame Commander's sentiments at the girl's sudden appearance.

"Oh, the same place he did," White Apple said. She pointed to the severe ten-foot-tall figure of Father Time, dressed all in black, who stood out from the rabble he incited even as he stood among them.

"Just a moment," she said. Leaning over to place her hand upon the deck Hanaawa appeared, unmoving and minuscule. As she drew her hand up and away, he grew in size until he regained his normal shape. When she pulled back from him, he gasped and became animated once again, staggering away from her and looking about in confusion and sorrow. Mrs. McClure and Seramis were nearest, and caught him before he fell.

"How did you do that?" Seramis cried out. "Please explain this—"

"I know we are due a conversation, milady," White Apple said quietly and respectfully, curtseying but maintaining eye contact in a most disconcerting manner. "But I'm afraid that it must needs wait, as I'm called to terrible purpose."

"White Apple! Please." Lady Seramis left Hanaawa's side and rushed to her, dropping to one knee. "Any purpose, terrible or fair, can surely be shared among friends?"

The maiden smiled. "Truly, you bring out the best I have to offer, milady," she said. "While whatever it is that Father Time has become brings out—well, maybe not the worst." Looking at the Prussian camp, she added cryptically, "Maybe not yet." A cruel and vengeful grin began to grow.

"You don't have to—" Seramis said.

Hanaawa interrupted as soon as he had recovered. "White Apple, you are to be the matriarch of our people! It would be wise to listen to counsel before—"

"I want to learn what it means to be powerful—what it feels like to walk into someone else's lands and wipe out entire populations without regret or recrimination. I want to know what it's like to be an unstoppable force in an alien land." She sighed, lost in thought for a moment. "However, unlike the invaders from this land who waged an undeclared war in my home, I'm part of this crew, under this flag, and we've declared hostilities, yes?" Her eyes flashed, and she stepped to the rail of the vessel. "Good-bye! Or, better perhaps, au revoir!" She stepped onto the rail and leapt over the side.

Rushing to the rail, Seramis and Hanaawa were too late; helplessly they watched White Apple dive towards the ground some four hundred feet away at what seemed to be an unnaturally high rate of speed. Her arms outstretched, she flew straight down, swooped into a somersault, and rolled into her landing upon the ground. Bouncing to her feet as she came out of the maneuver, she ran towards the Prussian camp.

Lady Seramis recovered her wits sufficiently to call out for the signal officer to warn the commanders. "A declared enemy in is making its way towards them," she shouted. "And tell them, too, of a dangerous friend in the form of White Apple, should they once again attack the Prussian camp." The lights flashed as the signal was relayed, and Seramis turned to her friends. "Once again, it looks like we have the same dilemma! Do we go to aid our friend White Apple? Or do we join the fight against Father Time?"

Captain de Ibarra had watched White Apple leap gracefully from the *Agility*, but it wasn't until he saw her in his field glasses as she strode into the Prussian camp that he caught sight of her again. He watched her clap her hands, then draw them apart, and the soldiers in front of her were tossed away like paper dolls in a breeze. "I don't think White Apple needs our immediate help," he said. He watched her wave at a fusillade of bullets, stopping them in mid-flight where they froze before falling straight down to the ground. Shaking his head in amazement, he could only mechanically describe the miracles he was seeing.

Colonel McClure also watched White Apple through an eyeglass. "How is this possible? Hanaawa, what has happened to your niece?"

Hanaawa nearly choked on his emotions. "I don't know if she is my niece anymore!" He sank to the deck. "I have failed her—"

"Please," Lady Seramis begged. "We may yet help. What happened?"

Recovering, Hanaawa whispered thanks before describing the godlike figures he had seen. It took only a minute to briefly report what had transpired in Ireland after the airship left.

"What?" Captain de Ibarra said after he heard the chief's news. "There are more gods to contend with? We don't even know what to do with the ones we have..."

Father Time had reached the Elbe and with a touch froze its surface, allowing his horde to cross the ice and avoid the bridges controlled by the English heavy cavalry. Once they gained the same side as the English and the Prussians, Father Time rushed his horde into a singular mass. "I've never had an army before!" he exulted, although what constituted an army to him was a mere mob to any other.

Small companies of English heavy cavalry with pikes, carbines, and armor charged straight at the horde, but turned away at the last minute just before Father Time would attempt to deal with the attackers himself. He then lost interest, while a portion of his mob raced after the feinting cavalry, only to be run down and ground into the frozen mud when the cavalry reversed themselves, regroup, and charge again. This happened several times before the tactical pattern became apparent to Father Time; with a wave of his hand, he knocked aside the riders as if swatting at insects but with deadlier effect.

Father Time had lost more than half of his army, but he still had a three-to-one numerical advantage over the Alliance forces now in defensive formation to the south of Lauenburg. Twenty thousand Prussian troops remained, and should they join with the rabble, the Alliance would surely fall.

"Friends," Lady Seramis announced as she surveyed the mob, "we can surmise that if Father Time and White Apple worked together, none could stand against their combined might, correct?" She waited for assent before continuing, but no one spoke up. "Hanaawa says that those who control Father Time have ordered him to sustain the fighting and prolong this war. That explains why he attacks the Alliance while she attacks the Prussians." She paused for a moment, thinking. "I have a plan for how to deal with Father Time, but it means that we are to be the bait!"

The *Agility* floated low over the horde, and the few among the rabble who had captured blunderbusses and pistols from the enemy took ineffective potshots at the airship as it swooped in at full speed. Fritz had returned to the field, now commanding the cuirassier regiments of the English heavy cavalry. Lady Seramis, using a horn to amplify her voice, called out to Fritz, but with every intention of being heard by Father Time: "Lead your men against the Prussian cavalry and crush them! We have a new ally who will keep their infantry busy!"

"Who is this ally? Have I been betrayed?" Father Time strode to the center of his mob, still out of range of the Alliance infantry. "Ah, is that the Helleborine girl I hear?" Then as if voiced from everywhere, all at once, he spoke the words of the poet: "*Come not within the measure of my wrath!*"

"Yes, it is I, false priest!" Lady Seramis shouted even as her blood ran cold in fear, while the Alliance cuirassiers rode out in a deafening charge. She had already signaled the plan ahead of time, as no one on horseback could likely hear her call. Of course, whether or not they actually engaged the enemy was immaterial; they simply had to look as if they were doing so. "White Apple told us all about how she fooled you!" Lady Seramis lied. "She wanted to be here to defeat you herself, but I disagreed!"

Livid, Father Time spat out his words. "All in war—with time—for love of you?" Incredulous and defiant, he hurled bolts of lightning from his outstretched hands. They discharged indiscriminately, blasting at his own mob as often as arcing out into the sky. Rolling waves of thunder crossed the plain and buffeted the crew of the *Agility*, but did no

The Fury of Storms

further damage as Lady Seramis instructed Captain de Ibarra to navigate around the areas where she could see charges were building up. In one close call, she felt the hairs on the back of her neck start to stand up before she dropped one of the emergency ballasts, shooting the airship up and away from the incoming blast.

"White Apple was right! You are weak, so-called Father Time! If she were here, it would be merely a matter of moments before you were dead and gone forever! I'm glad she isn't, as it would be a waste of time!"

With a wordless scream of rage and defiance, Father Time grew, but maintained his material form, reaching out slowly to crush the *Agility* with his bare hand, now itself twenty feet long from wrist to fingertip. But the aerial rudder spun the airship sideways, and from the open gun ports a broadside of cannons tore across the intervening distance in an instant to blast the gigantic adversary from close range.

The broadside should have torn Father Time in two, just as the artillery barrage that came from the English guns in Lauenburg at that very moment had that desired effect upon the front lines of the mob. Captain de Ibarra turned the airship away from the mob and the giant form of Father Time in its center. Unfortunately, he was still growing and still largely in one piece, although hideously deformed by the cannon shot that had exploded in his torso, leaving holes or indentations that were only slowly returning to normal, as Father Time apparently inhabited a slower time scale at this size.

That pause on the adversary's part gave the artillery time to lay waste to his ersatz army, scattering its components in all directions as its leader was distracted by healing or whatever else might be keeping him from responding at the moment. The infantry kept their defensive position, preferring to attack a military unit with a strategic objective and not simply pour their musket balls into an incoherent mob. Some of the crazed horde charged straight at the infantry, but were stopped by the English bayonets for their pains. Most ran back across the river to the Höhenwald, while some escaped in other directions. A few remained close to the monstrous form of Father Time because of a misplaced sense of self-preservation or loyalty, as his giant shape attracted the artillery gunners to set their sights upon him; now that they had his range, they pulverized the ground where he stood. Impervious to the cannonade, he grew still larger, becoming more and more immaterial as he did so.

Eventually, he disappeared, and King George II, who had joined his troops and stood out as the only officer on horseback amongst the infantry, shouted a joyous shout of victory, that—while deserved—may have been premature.

At that very moment, unseen by the king, just after Father Time disappeared from the battlefield, Lady Seramis gasped and flinched at his sudden appearance upon her airship, his ghostly form directly in front of her, clutching at her throat with both hands.

Chapter Fifteen: A Final Fight

In which conclusion and resolution are vastly different

Seramis recoiled from the apparent attack. She only had time to note that Father Time appeared indistinct—although threatening enough—before he materialized completely. And in that moment, he appeared in the position that she had just escaped. She thought he looked as if he had fully expected to be choking the life from her lithe frame with his own bare hands, and was taken by surprise to be clutching at empty air.

Seramis gasped as Father Time's appearance split into two. One, a hazy transparent outline of the wraith turned towards where Seramis had jumped and soundlessly moved his lips as if to shout.

Seramis wisely stepped back even farther, shouting a warning to her crew, "Repel boarder!" more out of caution than any hope that they could stop Father Time.

And then the real figure of Father Time followed as if the shadow had proceeded the actual form that blocked the light. In the next moment, Seramis saw Father Time turn towards her again shouting, "I welcome the punishment to come whatever it might be for confronting you like this—but know that I will kill you for it!" His utterance was cryptic in the extreme. *Punishment? For him? From whom?*

While speaking, the doppelgänger pulled a phantom dagger from an immaterial wrist sheath and threw it at

Seramis at the same time corporeal Father Time was threatening to kill her. The blade passed right through her just as Tempus was shouting "kill you," eliciting from her an involuntary scream of terror. She had moved to avoid the knife, but couldn't dodge it fast enough despite her swift reflexes.

However, the dagger was immaterial so she had escaped actual harm, diving to the wheel deck just a second too late to avoid its hazy blade.

But her dive to the deck in order to avoid the ghostly knife took place in the instant before Father Time pulled an actual dagger from his wrist sheath, in a move that echoed exactly what his hazy outline had just done. He threw the blade in precise imitation of his immaterial twin's actions, at the spot where Lady Seramis was no longer standing. It sailed out harmlessly over the rail of the *Agility*, at the same moment that Father Time's future echo screamed silently and jumped at where Seramis crouched. This time, she made no sound as she coolly stepped out of the way, completely unfazed by the ethereal assault.

"*There is no following her in this fierce vein*," Father Time cried out, again quoting the Bard.

She had no way of knowing how she was able to see Father Time's future movements. To the rest of the crew she seemed to be barely escaping Father Time's deadly attacks at the last possible second. Only Hanaawa had experienced anything like this, and he moved closer to be helpful if needed. He didn't want to say anything that might distract her if she was actually seeing where Father Time was going to be an instant before he himself arrived at that point in time and space, as Hanaawa had heard White Apple describe it.

Again, Seramis saw the ghostly image of Father Time's assault as she stepped away. This time casually wrapping her right fist with a kerchief, she planted her feet, braced herself, pulled back her arm, and made ready for Father Time to leap into the position just vacated by his ethereal form dropping to the deck like a rag doll. The instant Father Time appeared in his material form, Seramis punched him in the face where the jaw hinged, dislocating it and dropping him to the deck like he had never been hit before.

The ghostly figure pushed itself to its hands and knees, and Seramis positioned herself once again, this time drawing her booted right foot back and aiming a kick right where his groin would be. In the very moment the corporeal Father Time attempted to rise, she kicked him in his groin as hard as she had ever kicked in her life.

To the rest of the crew, Seramis had been jumping out of the way of Father Time's attacks and positioning herself right where he would be an instant later. The result was that she was incontrovertibly basting the villain previously thought to be unstoppable. An astonished silence fell upon the crew as they dared not even breathe while they watched the slight form of the Dame Commander kick away a flintlock that Father Time drew from within his leather coat.

Seramis hesitated, letting Father Time almost land one of his punches. He very nearly head-butted her when she paused for a moment. But in truth she was drawing out the confrontation as she had no plan for how to end this, mindful that the last time she had captured Patrick Tempus, he had slipped from his bonds like smoke.

Winking at Colonel McClure, who was watching intently and had nearly stepped into the fray on several occasions,

Seramis shouted, "Stay back! I don't know how much more of this I can take." She followed this with "He's nearly got me." Yet none of the crew, even Hanaawa and now McClure who were almost in on the joke—so to speak—dared move or interrupt.

Lady Seramis felt like she could do this all day, as she was exacting her vengeance for all the wrongs amassed since Father Time had become so twisted. Sparing her fist, Lady Seramis kneed Father Time in the face and broke his nose, whispering softly, "That was for setting your tool, Innes, against me." Bringing her elbow down against his kidney— she wasn't sure why such a creature as Father Time would feel pain, but she would take advantage of it as long as she could—she added, "That was for kidnapping me."

Seramis watched intently as one of Father Time's arms stretched impossibly long for yards and yards, in an attempt to snatch Captain de Ibarra's flintlock pistol. Gently pushing the captain out of the way, she said conversationally, "Excuse me, please!" She then grabbed two belaying pins and, slamming them together, crushed the fingers of Father Time's right hand. "That was for being a party to the destruction of Bermuda and the creation of this endless winter!" Seramis was confident now that she could defeat him—of course, provided that she could continue to see into his future.

She wondered about Father Time's future: did he have one? Would she be able to kill him, and what other end to this one-sided battle could she pursue? She had sought to defeat Tempus, and now that she completely dominated him physically, she realized that she had the power to extract justice from him. But besides this punishment, what could she do?

C.J. Pitchford

Dame Commander Seramis Helleborine had been in battle before, and that was what this was. She felt sick at it, but when she tripped Father Time while he scrambled to get away from her, she knew that she would have to proceed and follow through with the consequences just as any soldier would do. There was clearly no capturing him, and while he could've called out for mercy, apparently that wasn't in his nature. If he is going to fight to the bitter end, Seramis thought, I will see it through as well. She had grabbed a rope and started slipping knots onto the end of a makeshift noose. Father Time, despite his broken and bloody appearance, noticed this and saw his end coming as well.

Cutting a short rope free from the knot of the noose, Seramis pushed Father Time off balance, and quickly tied his hands. "Mrs. McClure, I require your pouch," she shouted. Sarah dutifully emptied it and handed it to her but had never imagined that her mistress would put it over Father Time's head. Seramis continued to push and trip and pull him off balance so as to distract him; she did not want him to slip away again.

Ignoring her nagging feelings of doubt she tossed the noose over a yardarm down on the main deck, where she subsequently pushed Father Time, who landed with a crunching thud. His ghostly precursors now went in many directions, as if there were numerous possible futures. Seramis paid little attention to them; she wanted to put an end to this as quickly and as definitively as she could.

Jumping down to the deck she called out for the crew to secure the rope, but to be ready to cut it—"If he doesn't hang for his crimes, I want him to fall!" Lady Seramis proclaimed as she put the noose around Father Time's neck. Kicking open a gate within the deck rail, Lady Seramis prepared to push her captive out into open air.

White Apple materialized at that moment. "You really shouldn't do that, if I may be so bold," she said quietly. In her homespun cotton dress, she appeared just to his left and pushed him back down to the deck to lie on his side. Recognizing her voice, Father Time laughed despite his broken nose and jaw, the muffled sound coming from within the makeshift hood. While he chortled, White Apple pleaded with Seramis. "I helped you to defeat Father Time, but please don't kill him!"

"What?" Father Time's laughter ended abruptly.

I haven't come this far only to be stopped so easily. Seramis jumped and pulled hard on the rope, strangling Father Time's laughter as the noose tightened, leaving only wet gurgling and choking noises to be heard as he was pulled up off the deck. Even as she tried to kill Father Time, White Apple's words echoed within her. "I helped you..."

"Please, milady," White Apple said as she slowly approached Seramis, who was not heavy enough to pull her victim completely upright and up off the deck.

"Why should I stop? Why did you help?" Lady Seramis shouted, and in so doing, her grip slipped. Father Time fell forward, almost pitching over the side. In fact, one of his hazy outlines did fall overboard at that moment, while others stayed aboard.

"Let it go," White Apple said, taking the rope out of Lady Seramis's hands and throwing it to the deck. The outlines disappeared; Seramis could no longer see the future timelines of her enemy.

From within the hood, Father Time cried out in a ragged voice, "Save me! Please!" And at the pitiful plea, Seramis's shoulders slumped. He continued without knowing the pity he had inspired. "Kill the Helleborine girl," Father Time shouted, "and all that I have and all that I can gain is yours!"

Seramis's eyes went wide in outrage, and she slugged the hood. "Stop, now." Surprising herself, she spoke words that came to her from nowhere. "*The croaking raven doth bellow for revenge!*" she called out, quoting the Bard as Father Time had done again and again.

Seramis looked aghast at White Apple as realization of her former ward's new powers dawned upon her. "Are... you going to kill me?" she asked in response to Father Time's pleas. She spoke hesitatingly, wondering at what had happened to the girl, and whether or not the situation had changed more profoundly than she thought possible.

"Of course not, milady!" White Apple said. "Not after I went to all the trouble to help you defeat him! And I don't think you're going to kill this creature, either."

"What is this? What new moral concept can you mean? This villain has reduced all we know—" Seramis started but was interrupted.

"It's nothing like that," White Apple spoke softly. "I hope you're ready for some answers—"

"I take it you already know the questions?" Seramis said.

"I think I know why you and Father Time are the way that you are—in one sense! I believe you and he were altered by invaders—"

"We? Are the same?" Seramis was repulsed by the idea, but she knew—in fact, she had directly experienced—the thirst for vengeance and had seen quite clearly the path that Father Time had chosen but she had avoided.

"No. However, you both were given powers at birth from a source that uses time as a weapon, by invaders that were in fact hoping that one of you would kill the other, as the resulting cataclysm would change the timeline and wipe out all life on the planet."

"I can scarcely believe this. How do you know that?" Lady Seramis struggled to understand—a situation most unusual for her, indeed.

"If you didn't already have the innate ability to manipulate your perception of time, I couldn't have opened that perception to see echoes of the future as I did. It was no more than... than... making an unheard whispered suggestion, is the best way I could describe what I did. And you were able to see Father Time's future as I can." White Apple smiled at her, looking as she had when they had first met, in spite of all the events that had happened since. "The rest I learned from the invaders who thought that I was the apprentice to Father Time and would help him to kill you, despite their warnings against such an action. They appeared to me before you fought Father Time—that was admirable work, by the way!"

"Thank you." Seramis shook her head in confusion. "Why do I feel like I've been passed by in teaching you, as you've certainly outgrown me?"

"Outgrown? Indeed! She has surpassed all of us," Hanaawa changed his expression, and spoke formally. "White Apple, within thee is the knowledge of all the powers of time and space. Thou art the matriarch of thy clan and have realized thy true potential. I have been present at both thy physical and spiritual births." The realization overwhelmed him. "The legends say that thou art immortal, the new incarnation of the Sun King!"

"I know that's the literal translation, Uncle, but I prefer Sun Monarch, please," White Apple said modestly but precisely.

He dropped to the deck in supplication. "I am yours to command."

"I prefer you standing, please." Lifting her uncle by the hand, she continued. "Although these are better in this diminished form." And she placed her hand on the deck as she had earlier brought Hanaawa forth, and two tiny golden figures appeared where White Apple touched the deck.

"Are those the gods Hanaawa described?" Seramis asked.

"These are no gods, milady—only rapacious invaders," the maiden said sadly.

She lifted her hands only a few feet, and the sky turned black. Teeny, tiny, tinny voices shouted, "We will rain destruction down upon you!" and "We shall eliminate every single one of you!" Like mad, despotic infants, they shouted and threatened helplessly. But Lady Seramis shivered when she saw them and was instantly afraid.

When the sky went dark at the appearance of the invaders, Captain de Ibarra felt the airship shudder. He grabbed the wheel with both hands and shouted to the crew, "Stations!" They had—with reason—been distracted by the confrontation between Father Time and Lady Seramis. While there was a lantern already lit at the wheelhouse, its feeble light didn't extend much beyond the aft quarterdeck. The main deck was lit by the invaders, but the crew lit lanterns at the foredeck and the mainmast.

The tiny beings continued to threaten and scold while the darkness grew about them. "Shush," White Apple said, as she pushed her hand down upon the diminutive shapes, but they resisted.

"Uh, oh!" White Apple said quietly.

"What do you mean, 'uh oh'—what is this 'uh oh'?" Lady Seramis asked. She, too, had felt the airship shudder, but couldn't see or determine their heading or direction through the inky blackness that surrounded the ship.

"Hanaawa and I have seen them previously," White Apple said conversationally as she attempted to manipulate time and space into a stable and closed geometry. "And they came to this planet at this point from outside of time—they travel in time to invade lands just as humans travel from continent to continent to do the same. They tried to force me into helping Father Time kill you, milady."

The diminutive forms were slowly being pressed together by White Apple's manipulations. "I had already learned where my power came from when they last appeared to me, so I amused myself for a while with them, but it appears they have a trick or two left." White Apple smiled and Seramis wondered if to one such as her this were a mere game.

But Seramis was more than a bit shocked to contemplate the possibility of traveling through time, let alone think that beings from outside of time itself plotted her destruction. "Why did they create me," she asked, "only to manipulate you into destroying me?"

"They didn't—exactly—create you and, well, they didn't want me to be the one to destroy you, either!" White Apple shrugged as she spoke. "But they did alter both you and Father Time, and if one of you should cancel out the timeline of the other, time itself would wreak such havoc as to destroy everything whose existence depends upon it." White Apple actually looked worried but Seramis wasn't sure she understood. "Everything that moves, breathes, germinates or what have you would have been extinguished, leaving this planet ready for the taking." White Apple patted Seramis's hand, both giving and taking comfort from the gesture.

Lady Seramis's knuckles were still tender, and she flinched at White Apple's gentle touch. She was reminded of the lump that was Father Time. She also noted the worried look on White Apple's face, but trusted that the girl had her new powers in control.

"Well, while what you say is scarcely believable despite my own part in it—in fact, it's perhaps the most far-fetched story I've ever heard—I will yield, of course, and not kill this pathetic creature." She indicated the fallen Father Time. "But what are we to do with him?"

"Oh, I'll take care of this," White Apple said simply while with one free hand she pushed time and space around the body of Father Time until he was gone, just as she was attempting to do with the invaders. Of course, Father Time was unable to resist, unlike the invaders who turned the sky dark and removed all light from the local environment.

"Will you take care of everything so neatly?" Lady Seramis said, in wonder at White Apple's manipulating matter and time as easily as solving an equation. It felt as if everything was falling down around her, but she dismissed the feeling.

"I think I've learned enough about these," the maiden admitted. "I've already known what it's like to be invaded, and I just learned what it means to invade. Now, it's up to me to repel invaders from outside of time itself." She smiled as she compressed the tiny beings still further. "Did you ever think I'd learn all that?" However, the invaders would still not yield. "I think I should try to take these with me. I have made time—well, slippery is the word I think is appropriate—for other travelers such as these. They will not be able to invade so easily. Oh, I would like to someday discuss all that I've learned with you!" White Apple said brightly.

Seramis hugged her. "Let us have that discussion someday, where I find if there's anything left I have to teach you, and I try to appreciate all you have to teach me."

"I should return to my home presently, as I want to know what has happened there since the war. You are welcome any time." White Apple looked warmly at Lady Seramis and the McClures. "But I don't know about the others," she said, winking at Captain de Ibarra.

"What?" he said. "What did I do?"

White Apple would have run to the captain to give him a hug, but they were both too busy; she waved instead.

"Is this how I should say good-bye to a Sun Monarch?" The captain asked and waved back.

"That's how I say good-bye to a friend," White Apple said.

"Adolescents! Why do they have to argue?" Captain de Ibarra said, failing to hide his tears. "Go on, now! Find your own craft to experiment upon!"

Turning to the struggling but diminished invaders, White Apple reached behind their shapes and pulled upwards, lifting reality itself, and into the opening pocket of dimensionless space she pushed them. Enclosed by the seemingly malleable fabric of time and space, they grew indistinct, helpless within the trap. Smiling, White Apple turned to Hanaawa. "Are you ready? Or perhaps should I ask first: are you willing to travel with me?"

"I'm not one to argue!" Hanaawa said, "Just give me a little warning before..."

"Never!" White Apple shouted playfully and grabbed Hanaawa, and they both vanished instantly, as did the invaders. As they left, so did the darkness. When the light returned, it returned in the form of the ground rushing up to meet them as the *Agility* was about to crash into the Prussian camp.

"Brace for impact!" shouted the watch and the captain as the latter instinctively slipped into the lashes meant to keep him at his post just before they hit the ground.

From the point of view of the combatants, impenetrable darkness had fallen on the battlefield without warning, and when it lifted as swiftly as it had come, it revealed an airship crashing down upon the camp of the Prussian army. Its massive envelopes of buoyant gas notwithstanding, it was heading for the ground at an alarming speed, sending terrified Prussian soldiers fleeing—those who still could run, that is—from the likely point of impact.

Captain de Ibarra, who had always thought of his vessel as a living thing in the decade he had been at the helm, tried his best to protect it as he saw the inevitable about to occur. While Seramis and the crew protected themselves, he threw the wheel hard over to change the yaw—the *Agility* was now going to crash on its starboard side instead of bow first—and he hit the last emergency ballast release, sending the craft into a roll up and away from the ground, but not enough to counteract its descent.

The craft hit the ground nearly on its side, its forward momentum transferred from the masts down through the decks and into the keel. It hit hard, spraying dirt and rock and Prussian infantry unfortunate enough to still be in the way. The lookout was knocked from the crow's nest, one of two lost from the *Agility* in the crash. The vessel actually rose after impact, as the gas envelopes pulled upwards. The airship might have returned to the air for good, except for the row of trees on the northern edge of the Prussian camp that it failed to clear and exploded clear through with a tremendous crash.

The vessel came to a hard stop on the ridge past the line of trees, and almost pitched its contents—the crew—from the deck as the superstructure holding fast the gas envelopes continued its momentum forward over before returning upright, as if it had piloted to a stop through the entire maneuver. Seramis jumped up to check on the crew, calling out to others before shouting for damage reports.

"Oh, Captain! Your quick maneuvers surely saved us as no other could—" But there was only silence in reply. "Captain?" she cried as she ran up the steps to the aft quarterdeck and the wheelhouse. "Captain?" she cried again, but her voice was ragged. The ground thundered and quaked as her own body shook in grief when she saw Ibarra's unmoving and broken form, still lashed to his position in the wheelhouse.

The Fury of Storms

Seramis rushed to him, hot tears streaming down her cheeks. Loosing the bonds on his broken body, she cradled his limp form in her lap. She could barely hear the bosun call for medical attention while Mrs. McClure also ran to his aid. She no longer felt the ground shake in her grief, but there was a violent rumble that surrounded the craft and thundered all about her. Crying, Seramis tenderly straightened the captain's broken limbs, and wiped clean his ruddy features. "You saved us," she whispered. "You saved me so many times..."

Ibarra's eyes fluttered open, and he weakly whispered through blood-stained lips.

> *"Had we but world enough, and time,*
> *This coyness, Lady, were no crime..."*

He quoted a love poem, as he loved his ship and his mistress and was saying good-bye to both. He was fading and in pain but comforted by Lady Seramis's presence. She held him, and sadness passed into acceptance.

The world around her grew dark once again, and she felt herself and the captain transported as the words she had spoken once at the ritual passing of Hanaawa's kin came back to her in a rush, which she now voiced in ritual cadence.

> *"From birth do we believe in lies,*
> *As we forget what is unseen by our eyes!"*

The only break in the darkness was the light—the essence of Captain de Ibarra—that began to flow free of the broken shape that was his body. Lady Seramis spoke words that seemed to echo through time and space.

"*Return to the truth from which you came,*
That part we all share, where we are all the same..."

The bosun and Mrs. McClure arrived at the captain's side at the same time, placing a small mirror next to his face along with a cloth damp with water that now would never be tasted. Seramis looked at the face and its reflection, and whispered good-bye again and again, but no cloud of breath appeared on the mirror—and she knew he was gone.

Still, the ground trembled and shook as Mrs. McClure helped Seramis stand and she looked around in wonder as she saw the English cuirassiers charge into the disorganized Prussian camp. For the second time in the battle of Lauenburg, the Prussians had been caught unprepared by English cavalry.

Seramis almost didn't care for battles, or for nations, as she turned to help her crew's fallen, but Mrs. McClure stopped her with a gentle touch. "There will be time to pay your respects, my dear, but there's work still to be done." Mrs. McClure pointed to where the standards for the cavalry regiments had appeared and were now headed towards the *Agility*. She wiped away the tears from Lady Seramis's face and hugged her tightly. "The captain was proud to serve you, as are we all. He would have wanted—had always wanted—us to do our part proudly and surely."

Seramis thanked her as she hugged Mrs. McClure, "But my responsibility to our dear captain is not complete." She then solemnly helped carry the fallen Captain de Ibarra while the colonel went to greet the standard bearers and the unequal battle raged all around.

"Hail, airship!" Henry Albion called out.

"Hail, rider!" Colonel McClure answered. Assisting in bearing the captain towards the foredeck, Seramis thought at that moment she had never heard a more welcome voice than that of Albion, requesting to come aboard.

The crew was busy with tending to the fallen and repairs, so Colonel McClure opened the gate in the deck rail and pushed a ladder down after securing it.

"Permission to come aboard? I ask for myself, and their majesties, the kings of England and Prussia!"

The crew turned at this, and two jumped forward to assist the monarchs aboard. When they gained the deck—young Fritz having the easier time of it in comparison to his uncle—the crew on the main deck all paused while Lady Seramis, Mrs. McClure, the bosun, and the surgeon carried the still form of Captain de Ibarra down from the wheel deck. The crew knelt in honor of their fallen leader.

Colonel McClure joined to assist the bearers, motioning an invitation for Seramis to step aside. "As you can see, Majesties," she said as she curtseyed briefly, "we are gravely diminished, but remain in your service." The men bore the captain to the forward hold, to lie in state until his final voyage should end.

Surprising Lady Seramis and the crew, the two monarchs also knelt, to both the Dame Commander and the fallen captain. King George II himself said, "We acknowledge our debt to you, hard won though it may be. Your losses will be honored in Westminster Abbey, unless there are other arrangements you wish to make." Lady Seramis nodded in acknowledgment, unable to speak at the honor shown by the kings, and they returned to their feet.

Fritz nodded again to her. "Thanks to all that you've done, we've captured my father during his attempted escape. He readily abdicated the throne, and I will force him to stand trial. You—of course—are not required to be present, but your deposition will be helpful, if we might humbly ask it of you." He pointed to the battle beyond. "General von Schwerin holds out, as he rightfully questions my father's abilities, but wrongfully doubts my resolve." In the same vein, he continued proudly. "We will soon have the day, nevertheless."

Despite their practiced superiority, both of the kings appeared in awe of Lady Seramis and her airship, *The Agility of Clouds.*

"As soon as we're repaired, we can speed you and a small number of your retinue to your capital, Your Majesty." Lady Seramis briefly curtseyed to King Frederick Wilhelm II. Turning to the English monarch, she curtseyed again. "If you wish, we can re-supply in Berlin tomorrow morning, and then we can return you and the general staff that can be spared from the fight to London, my liege."

"I'm most grateful," the king said. "But don't hurry on my account. I am savoring the anticipation of seeing the view from this craft on high!"

The bosun approached her, subdued but also astonished at the sequence of events. "It's incredible, Dame Commander, but the damage was not that extensive. Repairs are almost complete..." Distracted, he retreated mid-sentence to continue his work, only just remembering to add, "We will be ready to depart after a final check, milady."

Lady Seramis nodded in response. Slowly, as an idea previously only half-formed sprang complete in her consciousness, she turned to her royal passengers. "Your majesties, please excuse me, as I have an airship to pilot," she said, smiling. Both kings bowed gracefully in response. She turned to Albion, the object of her affections who appeared before her just as he had when they had first met in Lord De La Warr's Neo-Palladian estate. "Admiral, you have some skill in navigation, I presume?"

"Yes, milady!" he doffed his bicorn and smiled. "I would chart my course to wherever you find yourself—even to the ends of the Earth!"

"Then please join me on the wheel deck and share in the task, as we need not wait for the tide." Taking his hand, Seramis Helleborine ascended the aft deck as the setting summer sun returned to Europe in a brief appearance through a break in the clouds, its light softening the edges of their view, melting the landscape into shapes indistinct and warm while showing the way forward into the future.

To Be Continued in Volume Three of
the Helleborine Chronicles:
The Baroness Le Strange

(the First Chapter of Which Follows)

PART FOUR: The World is Yours

Chapter The Last: A Wedding

In which our players celebrate and speculate

Pennants and pancels, flags and standards, banners and banderoles of every imaginable shape and hue flew from every available point on Westminster Abbey and elsewhere in Parliament Square, whipped about in the wind that marked the tardy return of spring in the late days of summer to a world that had nearly died within the grip of winter. Water flowed from still-melting ice as the breeze swept clean the mixed smells of foetid vegetation and the sharp tang of petrichor.

No Londoner of any station wanted to remain indoors as the sun rose flaming into the sky over the celebration that was the victory of survival as well as the union in marriage of Seramis Helleborine and Henry Albion. Commoner and noble-born mingled freely, forgetting their station whilst rubbing shoulders amidst great crowds of tradesfolk and their families, turned out in their best and most colorful clothes in the height of the latest fashions.

The currents of air rose and fell carrying the cacophony of dozens of competing bands, orchestras, musicians, and minstrels whose horns, reeds, and drums waxed and waned and blended and clashed as onlookers became participants and broke out in spontaneous cheers. Like a flowing tide, the applause that called out the common focus of the celebrants, crowds, and musicians alike rode the winds. Their jubilant acclaim crescendoed as a procession of horse-drawn open carriages followed by cuirassiers and ceremonial knights arrived at the north transept of the former cathedral under the radiant stained-glass rose window. The new western towers—in the Neo-Gothic style by the architect Hawksmoor—were still under construction, the work having been halted during the recent deep freeze.

The three hundred and forty-eight years since the last Royal wedding were still not long enough to have witnessed a comparable spectacle at the Collegiate Church of Saint Peter at Westminster, as named by the Tudor Queen Elizabeth. Westminster Abbey overflowed with humanity as all London gathered to witness the wedding between the marchioness of Cambridgeshire and the duke of Gloucester, feted as the "heroes of Lauenberg" by some, "heroes of sea and sky" by others, but mistakenly called the "heroes of London" in an appellation that would be used by most. The advancing press of the curious and the grateful would have rendered movement all but impossible, except for two rows of musketeers clearing a path for the wedding party, led by the withered and grey figure of the elderly archbishop of Canterbury as they were about to process into the church.

The ceremony had actually begun earlier in a private chapel in the Palace of St. James, with only King George and Queen Caroline standing for Lord Henry, and Colonel and Mrs. McClure standing for Lady Seramis. It had been an informal and cozy affair, full of gentle goodwill and lacking all the grand pomp and rich circumstance of the current spectacle. But today's wedding wasn't the first ceremony held at Westminster Abbey since the Great Battle of Lauenberg.

Lady Seramis had returned to her homeland, and King George II to his capital, with caskets bearing the embalmed bodies of the late Princess Sophie Dorothea and former Captain Rogero Francisco de Ibarra y Valdez, and had laid them to rest only the day prior.

It had been the somber precursor, lasting all of yesterday afternoon, to the riotous explosion of sights and sounds accompanying this morning's brief ceremony. Today was the raucous and colorful version of the same conditions as yesterday, when all of London had then also turned out for the final entombment of Seramis Helleborine's fallen friends—but mostly to see the airship, *The Agility of Clouds*, floating at rest at its mooring.

The airship had once been a typical caravel redonda of the sixth rate, with its sails raked in the lateen fashion, and its main deck covering benches of rowers and cannons nestled between fore and aft quarterdecks. But most of the sails had been converted to great envelopes of pitchblende gas, allowing it to hover in the air—just as it was at the moment—tied down like a ship at anchor.

Today's winds lightly buffeted the small craft still attached to the scaffolding of the western towers of Westminster Abbey, but it was all but ignored as Albion stepped out of the gilt-framed carriage and turned to assist the Dame Commander, Lady Seramis.

Seramis looked at her groom's upturned, clean-shaven face and was instantly swept back in time to his proposal of marriage. They had talked incessantly as they floated from Lauenburg to Berlin, each filled with a sense of discovery and wonder at the love they found growing naturally between them. The only interruptions occurred when King George II drew Henry aside before disembarking in Berlin along with King Fritz (as he had asked his friends to call him), and immediately before Henry dropped to one knee in front of Seramis and the entire crew and declared his love and his intentions.

For his part, he intended to explore a partnership between her, Helleborine-Albion, and himself, Albion-Helleborine; the two of them would show the world the true meaning of love and freedom within devotion and exploration. The crew roared their approval when Seramis accepted, and King George II bestowed upon him the ancient title of Sea Lord while inventing an honorific, Lady of the Sky, for her.

A much louder roar brought Seramis back to the present as she accepted the proffered hand of her beloved. Despite— or perhaps because of—their thin gloves, Seramis could feel the heat of Henry's hand as it clasped her own. She felt her smile broaden as she looked into his twinkling blue eyes. She could think of nothing more welcome than those eyes as she stepped slowly upon the ground. As Seramis looked around, the tumult and the chaos of the crowd slowed even more with the wind-whipped pennants slowly undulating and pulsing, as if keeping time for Seramis alone.

But one figure moved to the beat of a different maestro. In the edges of Seramis's vision, in glances that inspired not concern but curiosity, she spied a fleeting glimpse of a swiftly moving blur as it swept into and amongst the celebrants. Seramis tilted her coiffed head to the side, her smile still in place, to look around the crook and miter of the archbishop, who was leading the wedding party into the church.

Henry raised an eyebrow while turning to Seramis. "What is it, dear?" he asked only just loudly enough to be heard over the cheering of the crowd. To her ears, he sounded languid and serene, as was usual except when he attempted to recite poetry.

Seramis slowly took in her groom's smile before answering. The gold of his sash and medals gleamed in the morning light as she looked up into his face, framed by oversized lapels and collars that were the latest style. "Maybe White Apple has returned to give us her blessing or possibly quiz us on married life? She could appear as anyone—any time—I would guess, and blend in as only a being of near limitless power can. She might even be trying to draw my attention in moving so quickly..."

Her voice trailed off as she resumed scanning the crowd. They had just entered the shadow cast by the church, and Seramis no longer felt the warmth she had felt since leaving the Palace. The incessant music, shouting and clapping reverberated against the walls of Westminster Abbey, rising in pitch and volume as the wedding party drew near to the entrance at the transept. But before the assembled celebrants reached the doors, a hush fell over the crowd. The silence spread from the opening of the church through the throngs as cheers fell from quizzical throats, melodies sank unsupported, and the syncopated rhythms dropped away one by one, until all were silent, except one.

One spoke in a contralto sure and steady, amplified by the natural shape of the entrance where she stood, in words that echoed above the crowd gathered in Parliament Square. "Your Majesty, not all Stanleys are Jacobites—we can be loyal and true!" the middle-aged woman said. Her words were guaranteed to gain the attention of everyone in ear-shot, causing a silence more profound than that resulting from the fall of any executioner's blade.

"Forgive me this plea; it is customary in Huntingdon and Peterborough that a family member call for the beginning of the celebration!" Raising her hands high above her head, letting her sleeves fall about and frame her face, which looked not unlike that of the woman she addressed, with the addition of but a few strands of grey in her piled hair, she continued. "I, Henrietta Helleborine, the Fourth Baroness Le Strange and the mother of the bride—"

"What?" gasped Seramis.

"—do joyously embrace and invite all who attend this union of man and woman within!" Her eyes shone as she finished, "Let the ceremony begin!" And she turned and strode straight into the great opening as the crowds redoubled their cheers, seeking to shake the very foundations of Westminster Abbey with their joy.

"Well and make no mistake," the elderly and frail archbishop of Canterbury said with a lilt in his voice as he turned to look at the party behind him. "May the Lord bless and keep us all, but I certainly didn't see that coming!" Unfazed, he then continued his shuffle towards the steps and up into the church.

Stunned, Seramis allowed her curiosity and the momentum of the moment carry her forwards. Her head was swimming in questions, but her surprise failed to mute her enthusiasm for the adventure she anticipated married life to become. With a brave smile to reassure her groom, Seramis turned and sought the eye of her king walking behind her.

"Cambridgeshire?" King George said. "I thought your mother—" Stopping sharply, he turned to his queen, silently opening his mouth in pain. She merely raised her chin an inch and both monarchs continued walking while Seramis turned her attention to lifting her train and mounting the steps to the church.

Seramis had thought, as did many, that her mother died when Seramis first drew breath. Long ago (so long she knew not when), she had stopped thinking of having killed her own mother as a child, of being responsible for her death. In fact, she had very nearly stopped thinking of her mother altogether. The guilt and pain she had thought buried now resurfaced as she prepared to leave maidenhood behind and become an adult, inexplicably blending with trepidation and astonishment at the appearance of the woman who strode confidently before her.

Her life had just been turned inside out, but more to the point, it had done so upon this day, the pivot upon which so many other things also changed. In fact, her entire world had changed yet again.

The Baroness Le Strange

George Frideric Handel himself conducted the wedding anthem, "This is the day which she hath made," recalling the coronation cantata, *Zadok the Priest*, in more than just spirit and theme—as much of the music had been adapted on extremely short notice. This time, the choristers didn't lose their place and sing out of turn (as they had in the Second King George's coronation of 1727), yet the effect as intended was just as dramatic and startling as the entire choir entered tutti forte with brass instruments loudly doubling their vocal lines.

As Seramis Helleborine and the rest of the wedding party walked down the North Transept past the Chapel of Saint Michael on the left and the choirs and orchestra in the nave further along to the right, the mother of the bride joined the party. Accompanied by a Fellow of the Royal Society, Edmond Halley, the newcomer curtsied and stepped into place behind King George and Queen Caroline.

Light from the high windows over the nave glittered on individual medallions and jewels as worn by the procession but failed to sufficiently illuminate the marble floors, making the wedding party appear to float on rays of light as they turned left toward the Chapel of Edward the Confessor, where the ceremony proper would take place.

The melodic lines of the choir singing 'amens' and 'alleluias' soared over the wedding party and audience alike just as the arches of the ceiling of Westminster Abbey curved to points high overhead. From outside, the cheers of all London could be heard through the open doors, while inside the audience clapped reverently but enthusiastically. The celebration of a simple union between two people had been transformed by an entire nation into a celebration of life's victory over death and a renewal of purpose and meaning.

But to Seramis, the entire proceeding was part of a larger ceremony that concluded one part of her life as she entered a new realm of adulthood and partnership. She followed the archbishop and matched the steps of her betrothed while not knowing exactly how to proceed—yet lacking the specifics at present wasn't a detriment when guided by tradition and shared purpose.

Her life's direction, it seemed, pointed towards more of a indistinct goal at this point than truly following an actual plan. In the past, she had worked upon the experiments that piqued her curiosity and attempted to meet what was expected of her as best she could. But she never imagined the sights and sounds that now surrounded her, nor did she ever aspire to an event like this as though now in the moment it seemed as delightful as anything she could possibly entertain.

The high altar in the chapel was full of admirals and captains from the Royal Navy, along with members of the households of Gloucester and Cambridgeshire. Of course, that included the crew of the *Agility*, so that nearly every continent and nearly every shape and hue of humanity were represented upon the dais where Lady Seramis and Lord Henry now stepped and knelt before the archbishop of Canterbury. As the anthem concluded with its strong plagal cadence and Handel, as conductor, lowered his arms, King George turned in an apparently improvised gesture and saluted the composer with his right arm held high. Instantly, everyone in the audience ceased clapping, and imitated the royal acknowledgment.

Such were the acoustics that even the frail archbishop could be heard throughout the cathedral when he welcomed all, raising both hands and speaking in a high voice, "We are here to celebrate the union of this man, Henry Albion, and this woman, Seramis Helleborine." He lowered his arms and his voice, and continued. "You will note that in the joining of these two people, there will be a joining of titles, of offices, of lands and of households, but we now focus on just these two right here and right now, so I repeat myself to emphasize the names and the persons here before us: Seramis and Henry. It is this simple and direct combination of two made one that we honor and cherish, we dedicate ourselves and our posterity for today and all days to come, for their love will be our love, their gains will be our benefit, their sacrifices our loss.

"We have all known grievous loss, and enter a new period of light and goodwill as we leave the darkness behind us. Like these two who humbly kneel before all, we also dedicate ourselves to a new union of all to all becoming all, just as they dedicate themselves for now and forever to a new union of one to one becoming one."

The archbishop raised a hand in blessing. "It is not from any one gift bestowed upon me do I offer a blessing to this union, but let all our blessings flow through this one offering, let all of us bless and support this union. Amen." He smiled. "I will have to resist the urge to continue, to recount the many highlights of this union, of these new opportunities within a new league of common purpose... It seems I am failing in brevity so pray allow me to yield to Henry, who would like to speak a few words."

King George II, standing next to the kneeling duke, helped Henry to rise. Henry thanked the king, and smiled at his family, friends and fellow officers. He nodded his head in appreciation before turning around to face the choirs and audience filling the nave and ambulatories. "God save England!" he cried out to cheers and ululations that arose from every corner of Westminster Abbey. "God save the King!" he continued, and somehow the tumult rose even higher. Turning to the still kneeling Seramis, he added, "And God save Seramis Helleborine, the Lady of the Sky, and my love!"

In the bedlam that followed, the Baroness Le Strange turned to her daughter next to her and said in a voice that only she could hear, "And if in failing that, pray that one other could prove useful in that stead, and be a savior if ever one shall be needed."

Seramis turned to her mother, eyes wide and struggling to understand how this reunion should come to be, here and now. She was speechless, torn by raw emotions, and utterly forgot her next assignment. She wasn't looking at her groom, who had turned to her in his planned introduction.

Henry Albion smiled, seeing Seramis evidently distracted by her mother, who was looking out at the assembled crowd, and continued on himself instead of introducing his new wife. "There is really, well, no more that I can say—at this point. I know that, umm, our time in this life is all too brief, and so I will be brief as well. But if I may add just one small dedication, please allow me to share with you all my own offering of love and lifelong commitment to this one remarkable woman."

The Baroness Le Strange

Seramis recovered and looked up at her new husband, tears brightly shining in her eyes. Henry reached out and lifted Seramis to her feet, holding her hand, he swept his other arm out and around in a flourish that brought every voice to a rousing cheer in honor and acknowledgment of the Lady of the Sky.

Time slowed for Seramis as she looked up at her new love, and basked in the warmth of his smile. She turned to her household standing behind the archbishop and saw Mrs. Persson crying in the arms of Mrs. McClure. She wished that her departed friend, the Princess Sophie Dorothea could have been there to comfort them as well. She realized as she thought this that she was thinking of the maternal love that she had experienced in her life, the caring and nurturing that she had felt from the women who had cared for her and had, for her part, tried to return that same caring—and she then turned to the woman who claimed to be, in fact, her actual mother. The woman who had given birth to her had supposedly died in that act, but looking at the woman who declared herself to be the last and lost Baroness Le Strange, Seramis felt herself torn by simultaneous feelings of joy and dread.

The crowd fell silent in anticipation of the next part of the ceremony, and Seramis turned to look out over the joyous faces, the smiles and tears of the thousands that filled Westminster Abbey. "I don't want to be saved," she said in a quiet voice that pierced the vast cathedral.

The crowd roared a mixture of astonishment and approbation.

"That is," she said, addressing the audience, "my ultimate salvation is something I must simply leave to a higher power, my own frail and humble faculties unable to divine such a purpose. I do not deny salvation—you all here are, in fact, witness to my new dedication and devotion." She grasped her new husband's hand all the tighter. "And I am eternally grateful for having been saved multiple times over by my love, Henry." She turned to her friends, "Thank you all for all that you've done. Your love shows me the true measure of support and sacrifice, and I hope to be worthy and share forward that same love for all the days allotted to me."

She turned to look at her mother, who slowly turned to look back at her. "I have been raised to gratefully accept and return the devotion shown me, and your love on this day will carry me through any trial or any burden that I will welcome should I ever hear the call." The baroness smiled at this, and touched the cameo locket she wore over her heart. Seramis recognized it at once, and her eyes grew wide as she looked at her mother with a new expression of wonder and amazement.

"In truth," Seramis said, smiling, "I can hardly bear the weight and power of the profound feelings within me." She turned to Henry, "Kiss me, my love. Let us show the world the true meaning of devotion."

As their lips touched, the voices of the thousands within Westminster Abbey erupted in joy. But a new note entered the din, as the rattle and clank of metal upon metal, the stamp of boots upon stones, and hoarse militaristic shouts shoved aside the cheers and the cries of goodwill with gasps of astonishment that bordered upon stupefication. At first, Seramis and Henry were lost in their kiss, the perfect moment that filled their whole being with such tender and absorbing love, that they were completely unaware—in point of fact, the last to be aware—that anything had changed at all.

The Baroness Le Strange

But the world for Seramis changed once again, as she broke the kiss with Henry and heard the sergeant-at-arms cry out, "Step away from Their Majesties! Prince William is missing and feared dead!"

TO BE CONTINUED...

www.ingramcontent.com/pod-product-compliance
Lightning Source LLC
Chambersburg PA
CBHW071130260626
47162CB00003B/739